Maxie Pichelsteiner was a most unusual boy.

First, and most important, he was slightly less than two inches tall. *Second,* since the death of his parents, he had been the ward of Professor Hokus von Pokus, the world-famous conjurer. *And third,* he wanted, more than anything else in the world, to be a circus performer.

Being less than two inches tall created problems for Maxie—like having special books printed the size of postage stamps so he could learn to read—but it also had its advantages. For one thing, it enabled the Little Man to fulfill his dream of becoming a circus performer in a rather unique way.

Erich Kästner's charming fantasy, translated from the German, will enchant readers with its wryly humorous style and imaginative theme.

THE LITTLE MAN

TRANSLATED FROM THE GERMAN BY

JAMES KIRKUP

ALFRED A. KNOPF / NEW YORK

THE
LITTLE
MAN

ERICH KÄSTNER

PICTURES BY

RICK SCHREITER

This title was originally catalogued by the Library of Congress as follows:

Kästner, Erich, 1899–
    The Little Man. Translated from the **German by James**
Kirkup.   Pictures by Rick Schreiter. ₁1st American ed.₁
New York, Knopf ₁°1966₁

    183 p.   illus.   24 cm.

    I. Title.

PZ7.K118Lic 2   67–2072

    Library of Congress   ₍8₎

Trade Ed.: ISBN: 0-394-81402-9   Lib. Ed.: ISBN: 0-394-91402-3
THIS IS A BORZOI BOOK PUBLISHED BY ALFRED A. KNOPF, INC.

First American Edition

© Copyright, 1966, by Alfred A. Knopf, Inc. All rights reserved under International and Pan-American Copyright Conventions. Distributed by Random House, Inc. Manufactured in the United States of America. Originally published in Zürich by Atrium Verlag as *Der Kleine Mann,* © 1963 by Atrium Verlag. Published in Great Britain by Jonathan Cape Ltd., © 1966 by Jonathan Cape Ltd.

THE LITTLE MAN

·1·

My first encounter with the Little Man · Pichelstein and the Pichelsteiners ·
Maxie's parents emigrate · Wu Fu and Chin Chin · Birthplace: Stockholm ·
Parents blown off the Eiffel Tower · The burial of two Chinese pigtails ·
Professor Hokus von Pokus delivers a fine oration

He was called the Little Man and his bed was a matchbox. Actually,
his real name was Maxie Pichelsteiner. But this fact was known to

very few people. And even I would not have known it if he hadn't told me so himself. That was in London, if I remember rightly. At Garland's Hotel. In the breakfast room, in fact, with all the pretty bird cages hanging from the ceiling. Twitter twitter twitter! One could hardly hear oneself speak.

Or was it in Rome? At the Hotel Ambassadore on the Via Veneto? Or in the dining room of the Hotel Excelsior in Amsterdam? I'm afraid my memory is going. Pity. Sometimes the inside of my head feels like a messy toy chest.

One thing, however, is quite certain: Maxie's parents and grand-parents and great-grandparents and even his great-great-great-grand-parents all hailed from the most foresty part of the forests of Bohemia. There is a high mountain there, and a tiny village, both of which are named Pichelstein. I took the precaution of looking it up in my old encyclopedia, where I found the following entry, set down in black and white:

> *Pichelstein.* Village in Bohemia. Population: 412. Com-
> munity of very small people. Tallest height 20 in.
> Causes of this unknown. Celebrated for its Amateur
> Gymnastics Association (Pichelstein AGA, founded
> 1872) and for what is known as "Pichelstein Beef."
> (For further details, see Vol. IV under entry "Econo-
> my Dishes.") For centuries, all inhabitants have borne
> the name "Pichelsteiner." Recommended reading:
> *Pichelstein and the Pichelsteiners* by the Rev. Alphonsus
> Funn, M.A., 1908, privately printed, O.P.

A queer sort of village, you may say. But I can't help that. The information given in my old encyclopedia is nearly always correct.

After one year of marriage, Maxie's parents decided to travel and seek their fortune. Small though they were, they had large ideas. And, as the village of Pichelstein in the forests of Bohemia did not offer much scope for their plans and dreams, the pair of them set out with bag and baggage—handbag and briefcase—into the great wide world.

Everywhere they went, they caused the greatest astonishment. People's mouths dropped open and they could hardly close them again. Although Maxie's mother was really as pretty as a picture, and his father sported a magnificent black moustache, they were no bigger than five-year-olds.

What had Maxie's parents in mind? As they were such excellent gymnasts, they wanted be become acrobats. And after they had demonstrated their stunts on the horizontal bar and rings before *Herr* Brausewetter, the ringmaster of Stilke's Circus, he applauded enthusiastically, clapping his white, kid-gloved hands and shouting, "Bravo, you little imps! I'm signing you up!" That was in Copenhagen. At the Tivoli Gardens. One morning, it was. Inside the "big top" circus tent erected on four gigantic poles. Maxie had not been born yet.

Although his parents had been leading gymnasts in Pichelstein, they still had a lot to learn through hard training. Not until three months later were they made members of the Chinese acrobatic troupe known as "The Bamboo Family." In fact, it was not a real family at all. And the members certainly weren't real Chinese, either. The twelve neatly-plaited pigtails that dangled down their backs were about as genuine as forged banknotes. But as "artistes" they were in the front rank and among the cleverest jugglers and acrobats who had ever appeared in a circus.

They would juggle with fragile cups and saucers, spinning them at the top of long, thin, flexible poles of yellow bamboo, so swiftly that the spectators could only gape in stupefaction. The younger ones would scamper like monkeys up smooth, long bamboo poles as thick as your arm, which were held upright by the biggest and strongest of the "Chinamen." Once at the top of the swaying poles, they would do handstands and, to the accompaniment of muted drum rolls, stand on their heads. Yes, and they would even do somersaults, a good thirty feet above the circus ring! They would flip head-over-heels in the air as easy as winking, and then, feet together, they would stand upright on the tip of the teetering bamboo poles and smile and wave to the spectators far below. The band would give three triumphant blasts, and the public would clap and clap until their hands were sore!

On all the posters and in the program, Maxie's parents were now billed as Wu Fu and Chin Chin. They wore artificial pigtails and brilliantly embroidered Chinese jackets and trousers of rustling silk. They traveled around with the rolled-up circus tent, the elephants and other wild beasts, the fire-eaters, the clowns and the trapeze artists, the Arabian steeds, the stableboys, animal trainers, bareback riders, mechanics, musicians, and Herr Brausewetter from one city to the next. They enjoyed great success, made money, and thanked their lucky stars, day in and day out, that they had got away from Pichelstein.

Then, in Stockholm, Maxie was born. The circus doctor examined him for a long time through a magnifying glass, smiled, and finally pronounced, "It's a boy! A fine, healthy specimen! Congratulations!" He was so infinitely tiny that the nurse very nearly threw him away one day with the bathwater. Fortunately, he yelled fit to raise the dead, and was saved in the nick of time.

When Maxie was six years old, he lost his parents. It happened in Paris, quite suddenly and unexpectedly. The couple had taken the elevator up the Eiffel Tower in order to admire the beautiful view. But no sooner had they reached the top platform than a great gale sprang up, blew them off their feet and, in a twinkling, swept them into space.

The other tourists, who were bigger, were able to cling to the metal framework of the parapet.

But it was all over for Wu Fu and Chin Chin. They were last seen, hand in hand, spinning away into the distance. Then they disappeared over the horizon.

Next day, the newspaper headlines ran: "Two small Chinese swept off the Eiffel Tower! Helicopter search fails to locate them! Sad loss for Stilke's Circus!"

Of course, the loss was saddest of all for Maxie, who had loved his parents very, very much. He shed many a tiny tear into his tiny handkerchief.

Then a Portuguese vessel fished a pair of pigtails out of the sea, south of the Canary Islands. Two weeks later, when the two pigtails, in a single ivory coffin, were buried at the cemetery, Maxie was so overcome with grief he felt he wanted to die, too.

It was a curious ceremony. All the circus people attended the funeral: the Bamboo Family in their embroidered jackets, the lion tamer bearing a wreath on his whip, the show rider, Galoppinski, on his black stallion, Nero, the fire-eaters with their blazing torches, Herr Brausewetter, the ringmaster, wearing his top hat and black kid gloves, the clowns with sad expressions painted on their faces, and finally, the person who was to deliver the graveside oration, the world-famous conjurer, Professor Hokus von Pokus.

At the end of his solemn address, the Professor said, "The two little colleagues we are gathered here to mourn today left their Maxie in our charge. Shortly before their ill-fated ascent of the Eiffel Tower they brought him to my hotel room and asked me to keep an eye on him until they came back. Today, alas, we know that they cannot come back. And so I must keep an eye on him as long as I live, and shall do so gladly, with all my heart. Is that all right with you, my boy?"

Maxie, who was peeping out of the breast pocket of the magician's professional tail coat, sobbed, "Oh, yes, Hokus! It's all right with me."

Everyone wept tears of sorrow and joy. Their tears made the make-up run on the clowns' faces. Then the Professor whipped five huge bouquets of flowers out of the empty air and laid them on the tiny grave. The fire-eaters thrust their torches into their mouths, putting out the flames. The circus band struck up the "March of the Gladiators." And then they all, led by Galoppinski on his black steed, Nero, dashed back to the circus.

For it was a Wednesday. And, as everyone knows, on Wednesdays, Saturdays, and Sundays there are matinee performances for children at reduced rates.

9

· 2 ·

*The matchbox on the bedside table · Minna, Emma, and Alba · Only
two ounces live weight, yet sound as a bell · The Little Man wants to go to
school · Trouble in Athens and Brussels · Instruction on the folding steps ·
Books as small as postage stamps*

Well, I think I have already told you that at night Maxie slept in a
matchbox. Instead of the matches such a box normally holds, it contained a tiny cotton wool mattress, a small strip of camel's hair
blanket, and a pillow no larger than the nail on my middle finger.
And the box was left half open, because otherwise the poor little
fellow would not have been able to breathe.

The matchbox stood on the bedside table next to the conjurer's
bed. And every night, when Professor Hokus von Pokus had turned
over to the wall and begun to snore softly, Maxie would switch off
the lamp on the bedside table, and it would not be long before he
was asleep, too.

The two doves, Minna and Emma, and Alba, the white rabbit,
in his wicker basket, all slept in the same hotel room as Maxie and
the Professor. The doves would perch on the top of the wardrobe.
They would hide their heads in their breast feathers and, when they
dreamed, they used to coo.

The three animals belonged to the Professor and helped him in his
performances in the circus. The doves would suddenly flutter out of
the sleeves of his tail coat, and he would magic the rabbit out of his

empty top hat. Minna, Emma, and Alba were very fond of the Professor, and they were simply devoted to the little boy. After the five of them had had breakfast in the morning, Maxie was sometimes allowed to sit on Emma's back, and then she would take him for a flight around the room.

A matchbox is two and one-half inches long, one and one-half inches wide, and three-quarters of an inch high. It was just the right size for Maxie. For even at the age of ten or twelve, he only measured two inches precisely, and just fitted nicely into the box. On the hotel desk clerk's letter scale he weighed only two ounces, yet he always had a good appetite and had never been ill. He had had the measles, to be sure. But the measles really do not count. Nearly every child has *them*.

At the age of seven Maxie had naturally wanted to start school. But the difficulties were all too great. For one thing, every time the circus moved he would have had to change schools. And often even change his language, too! For in Germany the teaching was in German, in England it was in English, in France it was in French, in Italy it was in Italian, and in Norway it was in Norwegian. The Little Man might well have managed even that; he was brighter than most children of his age. But the trouble was that his classmates were all of them much, much bigger than he, and imagined that being bigger was something special.

He put up with a lot, the poor boy. In Athens, for example, during the lunch recess, three little Greek girls popped him into an inkwell. And in Brussels, a couple of Belgian louts had stuck him up on the curtain rod. He had, of course, climbed down again at once, since even then he could already climb better than most. But he had not cared for such stupid tricks at all. And so the conjurer suggested to him one day, "Do you know what? The best thing would be for me to give you private lessons."

"Oh, wonderful!" Maxie cried. "When do we start?"

"Tomorrow morning at nine," replied Professor Hokus von Pokus. "But don't start grinning too soon!"

It took some time before they found out the most convenient way to arrange things. But gradually they solved their problems, and then, day by day, they began to get more and more fun from their lessons. The most important things, besides the reader and the exercise book, were a pair of folding steps and a strong magnifying glass.

In the reading lesson, Maxie would scramble up onto the stepladder's top step, because if he sat with his nose in the book the letters were too big for him. Only when he was perched on top of the steps could he read the print in comfort.

For writing, it was just the opposite. Then he had to sit at a tiny desk. The tiny desk stood on the big table. And the Professor would sit at the table and scan Maxie's scritch-scratch through the magnifying glass. It enlarged the writing seven times, and this was the only way he could make anything at all of the letters and the words. Without the magnifying glass, he and the room waiter and the maids would have mistaken the scratchings for ink splashes. And yet, as one could see quite clearly by using the magnifying glass, the letters were prettily and delicately formed.

The same procedure was used in the arithmetic lesson—the steps and the magnifying glass. And so Maxie was always on the move. Now he would be sitting on the steps, now at his desk.

One fine morning, the room waiter, who had come to take away the breakfast things, remarked, "If I didn't know for sure that the young gentleman is learning to read and write, I would certainly think he was taking lessons in gymnastics." They all had to laugh at that. Even Minna and Emma, who were perched on the wardrobe, chortled with them—for they were chortle doves.

Maxie did not take long to learn his letters. After a very short time, he could read as fluently as if he had been doing it all his life. And then he became, almost overnight, a bookworm. The first book that Hokus von Pokus gave him was GRIMM'S FAIRY TALES. And quite probably he would have finished the book within a week, if it had not been for those awful folding steps!

Every time he wanted to turn a page, there was nothing else to do but to clamber down the steps, jump down on the table, turn the page, then scramble to the top of the steps again. That was the only way he could proceed with the story. And after reading only two pages he had to climb down to the book again! And so it went on: turn the page, up the steps, read two sides, down the steps, onto the table, turn the page quickly, up the steps, read the next two sides, down the ladder, turn the page, up . . . It was enough to wear one out!

One afternoon the Professor came in just as the boy was crawling up the steps for the twenty-third time, tearing his hair with rage and shouting, "It's really awful! For heaven's sake, why aren't there any smaller books? With tiny letters?"

At first the Professor laughed at Maxie's bad temper. But then he thought awhile and said, "Really, you're quite right. And if there are no such books in existence yet, we shall have some printed for you."

"Is there someone who can do that?" the boy asked.

"I have no idea," the conjurer said. "But in March the circus will be playing Munich. Unruh, the watchmaker, lives there. We'll make inquiries of him."

"And why would Unruh, the watchmaker, know?"

"I don't know if he does know. But he might well know, because he often has to do with such things. For example, ten years ago he inscribed the poet Schiller's "The Song of the Bell" on the back of a postage stamp. And the poem is all of four hundred and twenty-five lines in length."

"Wow!" Maxie cried enthusiastically. "Books no bigger than postage stamps—just the thing for me."

Unruh, the watchmaker, did indeed know of a printing press which could print such tiny books! All the same, it was a costly little whim. But the Professor earned a great deal of money as a conjurer, and

Maxie's parents had left him their savings. So it was not long before the boy had collected a little library.

Now he no longer needed to do acrobatics on the folding steps. He was able to sit down and read in comfort. He preferred reading at night, when he was lying in the matchbox, and the Professor, after falling asleep, had begun to snore softly to himself. What a cozy atmosphere! Up on the wardrobe, the two doves would be cooing. And Maxie would bury himself in one of his favorite books; HOP O' MY THUMB, NILS HOLGERSSON, DWARF LONGNOSE or, best of all, GULLIVER'S TRAVELS.

Sometimes the Professor would mutter, half asleep, "Turn the light out, you little wretch!"

Then Maxie would whisper, "In a minute, Hokus!" Sometimes the "minute" would last for half an hour. But finally he would switch the lamp off, fall asleep, and dream of Gulliver in Lilliput Land, where the inhabitants looked upon him as a giant.

And this giant who strode over city walls and scuttled the enemy war fleet was, naturally, no other than Maxie Pichelsteiner.

He wants to become a circus performer · Big people and great people are not one and the same thing · A conversation in Strasburg · On the profession of interpreter · Through Maxie's obstinacy, the Professor's plan comes to nothing

The older the Little Man grew, the more often did they discuss his future. Each time he would declare, "I want to enter the circus. I want to become an artiste and I don't want to do anything else."

And each time the Professor would shake his head and say, "But my dear boy, that wouldn't do at all! You're much too small."

"Sometimes you say one thing, sometimes another," Maxie grumbled. "You're always telling me how many famous men were small. Julius Caesar, Napoleon, Goethe, Einstein, and a dozen others. You also told me that tall people are very seldom great people! Their strength goes to seed, you said, and when they are six and a half feet tall it doesn't leave much left over for their brains."

The Professor scratched his head. Finally he declared, "Anyhow, Caesar and Napoleon and Goethe and Einstein would not have made good circus performers. Caesar's legs were so short, he could hardly sit on a horse!"

"I have not the slightest desire to sit on a horse," the boy retorted irritably. "Were my parents bad acrobats?"

"Far from it! They were first class."

"And were they tall?"

"No, on the contrary, they were very small."

"Well then, my dear Hokus?"

"There's no 'well then' about it," the conjurer said. "They were small, but you are ten times smaller. You are *too* small! If you were standing in the ring, the public would simply not see you!"

"Then they would have to bring opera glasses with them," the Little Man declared.

"Do you know what you are?" Hokus asked grimly. "You are a big numbskull."

"No, I'm a little numbskull, and . . ."

"And?" the Professor asked eagerly.

"And I shall become an artiste!" Maxie cried, so loudly that Alba,
the white rabbit, let the lettuce leaf he was nibbling drop from his
jaws with the shock.

One evening after the circus performance, they were sitting in the restaurant of a hotel in Strasbourg, and Professor Hokus von Pokus was enjoying some truffled goose liver pâté. He nearly always ate after the performance because, if he ate before it, his tail coat became too tight. And that interfered with his magicing.

He concealed all kinds of things in his tail coat. For example, four packs of cards, five bunches of flowers, twenty razor blades, and eight lighted cigarettes. Besides these, the doves, Minna and Emma, the white rabbit, Alba, and everything else he needed for his conjuring tricks. With all that, it's better to dine later.

So now he was sitting at the table eating Strasbourg goose liver pâté and toast, and Maxie was sitting up on the table right next to the plate, letting himself be fed with tiny morsels. There followed a Wiener Schnitzel, fruit salad, and black coffee. The Little Man even received a sip of the coffee. Finally, they were full and satisfied and stretched their legs out in front of them—the Professor's under the table and the Little Man's on the table.

"I know now what you'll be," Hokus said, after blowing a wonderfully pretty white ring of cigarette smoke.

Maxie gazed in admiration at the smoke ring as it grew ever bigger and thinner until it was hovering around the chandelier. Then he said, "You've only just discovered it? I've known all along. I'm going to be an artiste."

"No," growled the Professor. "You're going to be an interpreter!"

"An interpreter?"

"It's a very interesting occupation. You can already speak German and quite a lot of English and French and Italian and Spanish and . . ."

"Dutch and Swedish and Danish," the Little Man went on.

"Quite, quite," the Professor broke in hurriedly. "When we've traveled around Europe with the circus for another couple of years you'll be able to speak all those languages even better. Then you'll take an examination in Geneva, at the famous Interpreters' School. And as soon as you've passed it, we'll set off for Bonn. A good friend of mine lives there."

"Is he also a conjurer?"

"No, he's something much better. He is a civil servant. He is Chief Information Officer in the German Federal Chancellery. I'll show him your Geneva diploma, and then, if all goes well, you'll become interpreter for the Foreign Office or even for the German Federal Chancellor himself. *He* is the most important and powerful man in the country. And, as he is often abroad and has to talk to other chancellors, he needs a really good interpreter."

"But not a Tom Thumb!"

"On the contrary!" the Professor retorted. "The smaller the better! Imagine he takes you to Paris, because he has to talk about something with the French President. Something very top secret. Something frightfully important. But because the German Chancellor can't understand French very well, he needs a translator who can explain to him what the French President is saying."

"And he has to ask me, of all people?"

"Yes, indeed, my Little Man," the Professor went on. He was very much taken with his idea. "You set yourself in the Chancellor's ear and whisper to him in German whatever the President says in French."

"But I'll always be tumbling down," Maxie said.

20

"No. In the first place, perhaps he has such huge ears that you can sit right inside."

"And in the second place? What if he has only very tiny ears?"

"Then he'll hang a fine gold chain around his earlobe, and you'll seat yourself on the chain. You'll be known as Counsellor Extraordinary Maxie Pichelsteiner and people will refer to you with bated breath as 'the official who has the Chancellor's ear.' Wouldn't that be nice?"

"No!" Maxie cried loudly. "I should find it horrible! I won't be any Little Man in anyone's ear. Neither in Germany nor in France nor at the North Pole. You've forgotten the main thing."

"And what is the main thing?"

"I'm going to be an artiste."

∘4∘

The Little Man wants to become a lion tamer · Lions are cats, aren't they?
Adventure with minced meat and whip · Maxie in the toothbrush glass ·
Report of an extraordinary game of football · Hokus jumps
through a flaming hoop

When the Stilke Circus was once again playing in Milan, Maxie excitedly said, on the third day, "Hokus, listen, the hotel cat has kittens. Four of them. They're eight weeks old and in room 228. They're jumping from the chairs to the table, then when they're on the table they jump down again."

"Well now," Professor said, "I think that's very sensible of them. They couldn't stay on the table forever!"

But today the Little Man was in no mood for jokes. "The maids showed them to me," he went on eagerly. "They are striped, and look just like little tigers."

"Did they scratch you?"

"Not at all!" the boy assured him. "In fact, we got on very nicely together. They were purring, and I fed them with some chopped meat."

The Professor looked at him out of the corner of his eye. Then he asked, "What are you leading up to? Eh? What have you got up your sleeve? Out with it!"

Maxie took a deep breath and, after a pause, declared, "I'm going to train them and present them in the circus."

"Who, the maids?"

"No!" the boy cried in exasperation. "The kittens!"

Taken aback, Hokus von Pokus sat down on the chair and was silent for two or three minutes. Finally he shook his head, sighed, and said, "It is impossible to train cats. I thought you knew that."

Maxie smiled confidently and then asked, "Aren't lions cats?"

"Yes, yes. They belong to the hunting cats. You're quite correct there."

"And tigers? And leopards?"

"They are also hunters, members of the great cat family. Quite correct again."

"When the tamer commands, don't they sit on high pedestals? Don't they jump through hoops?"

"Even through flaming hoops," the Professor agreed.

The boy rubbed his hands gleefully. "There you are!" he cried triumphantly. "If it's possible to train such big cats, it should be all the more possible to train kittens."

"No!" the Professor firmly stated. "It's quite impossible!"

"And why not?"

"I have no idea."

"But *I* know the reason," Maxie declared haughtily.

"Well?"

"Because no one has tried it yet!"

"And you want to try?"

"I do! I've already thought of a name for the act. The posters will read: "Maxie and His Four Kittens, Breath-taking Animal Training Act, Presented for the First Time!"

"Perhaps I'll appear wearing a black mask! And I'll also need a whip to crack. But I have one already. I'll use the whip on my old toy stagecoach."

"Well, I wish you luck, my young friend," Hokus von Pokus said, and opened his newspaper.

The very next morning, the maids put four low stools in room 228. The four little kittens sniffed inquisitively around the stools, but soon toddled back to their basket and rolled themselves up in sleepy balls.

Then the room waiter appeared. In his left hand he was carrying a plate and in his right hand he held Maxie. And the latter was holding in *his* right hand the lacquered toy whip and in his left hand a sharp toothpick. "To keep the wild beasts at bay," he explained. "In case they should attack the trainer. And to stick the meat on."

"Shall I stay with you?" the friendly waiter asked.

"No, thank you," the Little Man replied. "That would interfere with the training. It would distract the animals."

So the waiter went away. The trainer was left alone with his four victims. They blinked their eyes at him, yawned soundlessly, stretched, and began to lick each other as if they hadn't washed for a week.

"Now listen and get this straight," the boy shouted sharply. "This lazy life has got to stop. From today on, you're going to work. Is that clear?"

They went on washing each other and behaved as if they were hard of hearing. He gave a whistle. He clicked his tongue. He stuck the lacquered whip under his arm and snapped his fingers. He stuck the toothpick under the other arm and clapped his hands. He cracked his whip. He stamped his foot. The cats didn't even prick up their ears.

Only when Maxie, using the toothpick, had maneuvered a few bits of meat onto the footstools did the four come to life. They hopped out of the basket, jumped on the stools, gobbled up the bits of meat, licked their lips, and gazed expectantly at their trainer.

"That's the way," he cried enthusiastically. "Bravo! Now you must sit up and beg. Alley-oop! Forepaws in the air!" He pointed upwards with his whip.

But the kittens must have misunderstood him. Or else they had smelled that there was more chopped meat in room 228. Anyhow, they dived off the stools, made a beeline for the dish, and began eating as if they were on the brink of starvation.

"No!" yelled the Little Man, infuriated. "Leave that alone! This minute! Can't you hear what I'm saying?"

They could not hear. Even if they had wanted to. And they did not want to in the least. They lapped at the dish till it shook.

Maxie was shaking even more. But he was shaking with rage. "You get your chopped meat afterwards! First you must stand on your hind legs! And march in single file! And jump from one stool to the next! Do you understand?" He rapped the dish with his whip.

Then one of the cats snatched the pretty lacquered whip away from him and bit it in two!

As Professor Hokus von Pokus, deep in thought, was coming along the hotel corridor, he heard squeals for help coming from room 228. He threw the door open, looked about him, and began to laugh.

The four cats were sitting under the sink, gazing excitedly in the air. Their little whiskers were bristling. Their little tails were beating the floor. And up above, on the edge of the sink, Maxie was crouched in a drinking glass, weeping. "Help me, Hokus!" he called. "They want to gobble me up!"

"What nonsense!" the Professor retorted. "You're not made of chopped meat, after all! And you're not a mouse, either!" Then he fished the boy out of the glass and examined him thoroughly, back, front, and sides. "Your clothes are a little torn, and you have a scratch on your left cheek. That's all."

"What a lot of hooligans," Maxie complained. "First they broke my whip and chewed the toothpick to pieces, and then they played soccer!"

"Soccer? With what?"

"With me! Oh, Hokus, they tossed me in the air and caught me again and shot me under the bed and hauled me out again and dribbled me over the floor. Then they booted me into the air again and shot me under the bed again and pulled me out and bundled me under the carpet and fished me out again. It was frightful! If I hadn't caught hold of the towel and clambered up to the sink and into the drinking glass, heaven knows if I'd be alive now to tell the tale!"

"Poor old fellow," the Professor said. "But it's all over now. I'll bathe you and put you to bed."

The four kittens blinked spitefully at the Professor. They were vexed that the big man had taken away their little ball that gave such splendid yells when they played with it. Then they stretched their hind legs, trotted over to the dish, and stuck their noses in it. But the dish had been completely licked clean.

The smartest of the four thought, "Too bad!" and curled up like a pretzel on the bedside rug. Just before he dropped off, he thought, "I can only eat when someone brings something. Sleeping is easier. Because I don't need anyone to do that."

Meanwhile, Maxie was sitting woebegone in his matchbox, with a Band-Aid on his cheek, drinking hot chocolate out of his tiny, Meissen porcelain cup.

The Professor had stuck a watchmaker's glass in his eye and was mending the tears in Maxie's clothes.

"So you're quite positive one can't train cats?" the Little Man asked.

"Quite positive."

"Are they more stupid than lions and tigers?"

"No question of it!" the Professor said decisively. "They simply don't enjoy it. I can well understand why. *I* wouldn't enjoy jumping through flaming hoops, either."

Maxie couldn't help laughing. "That's a real shame! Just imagine! Only animals for spectators! Kangaroos and bears and sea lions and horses and pelicans! Just think of that! All seats sold out!" In sheer enjoyment, he pulled his hair and shouted, "There! Now you make up the next part of the story!"

"Very well," said the Professor. "In the orchestra pit, the elephants blow a trumpet blast. Then the lion enters the ring. He has a whip in his paw and a top hat on his golden mane. Suddenly there is dead quiet. Four solemn tigers drag a cage into the ring. Inside the cage sits a man in a tail coat, growling."

"Marvelous!" Maxie rubbed his hands. "And the man is *you!*"

"That's right. The lion sweeps off his top hat with a flourish, bows and cries, 'And now, ladies and gentlemen of the animal kingdom, we have the greatest attraction on our program! I have succeeded in taming a man. He is a very well-educated person. His name is Professor Hokus von Pokus. Before your very eyes, ladies and gentlemen, he will jump through a flaming paper hoop! I beg the woodpeckers in the band to favor us with a muted drum roll!' The woodpeckers begin drumming. The cage opens. Two tigers hold a hoop in the air. The lion cracks his whip. I emerge slowly from the cage and snarl. The lion cracks his whip again. I climb on the pedestal and snarl again. A glowworm sets the hoop on fire. It begins to flame. With a flick of his whip, the lion lashes the seat of my trousers. I roar with rage. He lashes me again. And then, with one great lunge, I leap through the blazing hoop. The paper bursts. The flames dance. I've done it! The elephants trumpet. The woodpeckers drum. I get up off the sand, dust my trousers, and give a deep bow."

"And all the animals in the circus clap like mad," the Little Man shouted excitedly, "and the lion rewards you with a veal cutlet!"

"And now you're going to sleep, young man!" the Professor ordered. He looked at his wrist watch. "It's Wednesday, and I must go for the afternoon performance."

"Happy conjuring," said Maxie. "But there's just one thing more."
"What's that?"
"Nothing could be done, unfortunately, with the four cats."
"No."
"But one thing's quite certain. I'm going to be an artiste."

A window-shopping expedition and a tailor's dummy · The shop assistant faints · After all, a gentlemen's outfitters is not a hospital · The difference between a statesman and a milkman

One hot day in July, the pair were strolling leisurely through the western sector of Berlin, looking at the window displays. Actually, it was only the Professor who was walking. Maxie was not strolling at all, but was standing in the breast pocket of the Professor's jacket. He had propped his arms on the edge of the pocket, as if the pocket were a balcony, and showed special interest in the windows of toy shops, delicatessens, and book shops. But things didn't always go to his liking. The Professor also enjoyed looking at displays of shoes, shirts, ties, cigars, umbrellas, wines, and everything under the sun.

"Don't keep standing such a long time in front of this drugstore," the boy pleaded. "Let us walk on and look at other things."

"Us?" Hokus asked. "What do you mean—*us?* To the best of my knowledge, only one of us is walking, and that is I. Are *you* walking? No sign of it, old fellow. You are not walking. You are being walked. I've got you well in hand."

"You haven't," the little imp retorted. "You have me in your pocket!"

They couldn't help laughing at that. And people turned around to stare. A plump Berliner nudged his wife and murmured, "There's a funny thing, Rieke! That man's laughing with two voices!"

"Well, let him have his little joke!" Rieke replied. "Perhaps he's a ventriloquist."

Again the Professor stopped, this time outside a window displaying gentlemen's wear. He looked at the tailor's dummies in their fine suits, walked on a few steps, turned back, examined the window display again, fell into deep thought, gave three vigorous nods, and said to himself out loud, "That's not such a silly idea!"

"What isn't such a silly idea?" Maxie asked, curious.

However, the Professor did not reply, but strode right away into the shop and told the dapper assistant, before the latter could open his mouth, "I would like the navy-blue suit in the window. The single-breasted one at 295 marks."

"Very well, sir. But I don't think it will fit you."

"That doesn't matter," the Professor muttered.

"Perhaps a few alterations may be necessary," the assistant suggested politely. "I'll ask the tailor to come down from the workshop."

"He needn't bother."

"It will take only a short time, sir."

"If he doesn't come down, it will take even less."

"But our firm sets great store on giving its customers satisfaction," the assistant remarked, slightly nettled.

"That's very creditable," the Professor said. "But I don't want to wear your navy-blue suit! I just want to buy it!"

"In that case, I would advise that the gentleman for whom the suit is intended should kindly pay us a visit," the assistant suggested. "Or, if you would give us his address, we could send our tailor to his house. We can do it this very afternoon." He pulled out his notebook in order to write down the address.

The Professor shook his head violently. "Your navy-blue suit out there in the window is intended neither for myself nor for any other living creature."

The assistant turned pale and retreated a step. Then he moaned, "Not for any living creature, sir? Then it's for—for a dead man? Oh!" He drew a deep breath and proceeded, "May I ask for the measurements of the—the dear departed? Even for a dead man—the suit must fit, more or less. Or else one of our tailors could be . . ."

"Nonsense!" the Professor answered brusquely. Then he calmed down again. "Naturally, you don't know what it's all about."

"It would appear so," admitted the assistant, completely frightened by now. He was holding on tightly to the counter, because his knees were knocking. The poor fellow was shaking like custard pudding.

"The important thing is that the suit fits your display dummy. It does, doesn't it?"

33

"Of course, sir."

"What I want is to buy the dummy along with the suit," the Professor explained. "Without the dummy, the suit is of no interest to me."

Before the assistant had time to recover a little, there piped up a small voice which he had not heard until then, "But why do you need the big dummy with the blond moustache?"

The assistant gaped thunderstruck at his customer's breast pocket. Maxie nodded amiably at the man and said, "Please don't be alarmed!"

"But!" the assistant whimpered. "First a suit for a dead man along with the dummy in the window, and now a little imp in the jacket pocket—it's too much!" He rolled his eyes and disappeared behind the counter.

"Is he dead?" the boy asked.

"No, he's only fainted," Hokus answered, and beckoned to the manager.

"And what do we need a tailor's dummy for?" the little fellow asked.

"I'll tell you later," said Hokus.

After the manager had hoisted his assistant onto a chair, the Professor again made his wishes known. "I should like to buy the navy-blue, single-breasted suit, along with the dummy wearing it. Also the shirt he has on, the tie, the suspenders, the shoes, and the socks. How much is all that, please?"

The manager replied unsteadily, "I don't know exactly, sir."

The assistant moved his pallid lips and stammered out, "512 marks. One per cent discount for cash payment. Leaving 506 marks, 88 pfennigs." It was obvious he was a most capable assistant. Then he slithered off the chair.

"He's fainted again," declared Maxie, matter-of-factly.

When the manager heard the new voice and saw the little boy in the breast pocket, he went cross-eyed, and grabbed desperately at the back of the chair.

"Is that gentleman going to faint also?" Maxie inquired hopefully.

"It's to be hoped not," the Professor said. "After all, a gentlemen's outfitters is not a hospital."

Well, the manager and his assistant recovered. The purchase was made. A taxi was summoned. The car's roof was slid back and, held by the Professor, the tailor's dummy stood upright in the vehicle.

"That fellow standing up looks like a foreign statesman on a state visit!" cried one Berliner as the taxi drove past.

"He can't be a statesman," another declared.

"Why not?" the former asked. "Who else would stand up in a car, as if it hadn't any seats?"

"He's definitely no statesman," the other repeated obstinately. "He's not smiling, and he hasn't waved at us once. And he would have to do those things if he were a statesman. We would have to be well aware of how tremendously pleased he is to be in Berlin and unable to sit down. Otherwise he's no statesman."

The car stopped at the crossing and the two Berliners trotted over towards it to settle their argument. But, before they reached the taxi, the light turned green and they were left standing in the middle of the street.

"Besides, no statesman ever travels in a common taxi," the man continued. "Either sitting or standing."

"I've never been for a ride in a taxi," the other said.

"If you had, that wouldn't make you a statesman!"

"No, I'm a milkman."

◦ 6 ◦

Agitation at the Hotel Kempinski · Herr Hinkeldey suddenly misses all kinds of things, gets them back again, and takes to his heels · What was Hokus before he became a conjurer? · And why did he buy the display dummy?

At the Hotel Kempinski, too, where Professor Hokus von Pokus was staying, a few eyebrows were raised. People there had gradually become used to the Little Man who slept on the bedside table in a matchbox. But the hotel manager and the doorman became distinctly nervous now that they saw a tailor's dummy being carried by two hotel porters through the lobby of the hotel.

Hardly had the dummy been set down in the middle of the Professor's room than the manager burst in, gazed reproachfully through his horn-rimmed glasses, and demanded to know the meaning of all this.

"The meaning of all what?" the Professor replied amiably, as if he couldn't understand what all the excitement was about.

"The display dummy."

"I need it for professional reasons," Hokus explained. "Concert pianists and singers bring their own grand pianos into the hotel with them, when they are on a concert tour, and play and make all kinds of noise for hours on end. They are artists and have to practice. I am a conjurer. I also must practice! And I don't make nearly as much uproar as my musical colleagues." He took hold of the manager's jacket and slapped him jovially on the shoulder. "What are you so concerned about, my dear fellow?"

"It's all getting too much for us!" the manager groaned. "Your Maxie and the two doves and the white rabbit and now this wooden dummy in a blue suit . . . ."

In a fatherly manner, the Professor put his arm across the manager's shoulders. "Don't be so tragic about it! My dummy requires no bed. He needs no towels. He won't burn the rug with cigarettes. He won't complain to the maids . . . ."

"That's all very true, Herr Professor," the manager agreed. "But after all, you only booked a single room! And now you are living in it with the Little Man and three animals and a tailor's dummy! That makes, all told, five extra persons!"

"Oh, so that's the way the wind's blowing," the conjurer said smiling. "Would you agree to the overcrowding of your charming room with the southern view if I pay you five extra marks a day?"

"That sounds reasonable," the manager hesitantly replied. "May I convey your kind offer to our cashier?"

"You may!" the Professor replied, and added, warmly shaking the man's hand, "You'd better make a note of it at once. Here is my fountain pen."

"Thank you very much. I have a ball-point pen and notebook on me always. They are part of my job. They are my tools, in a sense." The manager's hand dived into his jacket. He searched and searched and could find nothing. "Extraordinary," he muttered. "No notebook! No ball-point pen! I can't have left them in my office. It would be the first time in my life I'd done so." And he went on searching his pockets. Suddenly he turned as white as a sheet and whispered, "My wallet's missing, too! There was a lot of money in it!"

"Now calm down," said Hokus. "You'd better sit down and smoke a cigarette! You may offer me one, too. I feel like a smoke."

"With pleasure," the manager said, and felt immediately in his

39

right pocket. Then in the left. Then in his trouser pockets. His face grew longer and longer. "I've forgotten them, too," he stammered. "My cigarette case. And my gold lighter, both missing."

"Allow me," the Professor said, and brought out a cigarette case and a gold lighter.

The manager looked at the Professor in bewilderment.

"What's the matter? Have you lost something else?"

"Please forgive me for suggesting it," the manager said jerkily, "but might it be possible that the cigarette case and the lighter do not belong to you at all, Herr Professor—but to me?"

Hokus looked closely at the two objects and said in perplexity, "Really?"

"My monogram should be engraved on the case, a 'G' and an 'H'. Gustav Hinkeldey. That is my name."

"A 'G' and an 'H?' " the Professor said, examining the case. "That's right, Herr Hinkeldey." He immediately returned the objects.

"I must really beg your pardon for making so bold as to draw your attention to . . ." the manager began in some confusion.

"Not at all, not at all, Herr Hinkeldey! If either of us is to blame, it is I! So please excuse me—you know, sometimes I'm so absent-minded, I put things in my pockets which don't belong to me at all." The Professor cautiously patted his pockets. "Why, there's something else here!" he exclaimed in astonishment, and produced a notebook and a ball-point pen. "Perhaps these things are also your property?"

"Yes, indeed!" Herr Hinkeldey said eagerly, and snatched them both. "I just couldn't understand how I didn't have my notebook with me." Then he was silent and thoughtful until finally he asked, suspiciously, "In your absent-mindedness, did you also, perhaps, slip my wallet into your pocket?"

"I should very much hope not!" the Professor replied, feeling himself all over. "Or can this be it?" He waved a black morocco-leather wallet in his left hand.

"Yes, it is!" the manager shouted, grabbed it, and started for the door, as if he were afraid the wallet might disappear again.

"Is the money still inside?" Hokus asked, highly amused.

"Yes!"

"Please, count the notes! I should not like you to complain later that some of them are missing. Put on your horn-rimmed glasses and count it all carefully!"

"My glasses? I've already got them on," Herr Hinkeldey said.

Only when the Little Man began to laugh, and went on laughing more loudly and heartily, did Hinkeldey stop, grab at the bridge of his nose, and then let his hand drop in perplexity. "Where have they disappeared to?"

"Now, where does one put one's glasses when one takes them off without thinking?" the Professor asked helpfully. "I wouldn't know because I myself have never worn glasses. Have you got them in your case?"

The Little Man was almost choking with laughter. "Stop it, Hokus!" he cried ecstatically. "I can't bear any more! I'll fall out of your breast pocket if I don't stop laughing!"

The manager gave him a scowl. "What's so funny?" he growled. Suddenly it dawned on him—his glasses were on the Professor's nose!

41

With one movement he snatched off the glasses, rushed to the door, and yelled, "You're a devil!"

"No, he's a conjurer, Herr Hinkeldey."

But the manager was in no mood for any more conversation. He flung open the door and shook the dust of the room from his feet. (Although in such well-kept hotels as this, there is no dust lying about anywhere.)

After Maxie had somewhat recovered from this joke, he said admiringly, "Herr Hinkeldey is quite right. You're a devil. I've seen you at it often enough in the circus, when you bring two or even three people out of the audience and empty their pockets without their noticing a thing! How do you do it?"

"One simply has to keep on talking to them nicely," Hokus said. "One has to keep patting them on the shoulder in a friendly way. One has to buttonhole them. One has to pretend to be brushing a shred of tobacco or a piece of thread from their clothes. The rest is not all that difficult once one has learned how."

"And how did you learn? And where? Just hold me up against your ear a moment, will you? I must ask you something very, very quietly." The Professor carefully extracted the Little Man from his breast pocket and held him to his ear. "Dear Hokus," Maxie whispered. "You can trust me. I'll definitely not let it go any further. Were you perhaps, earlier in your life, a pickpocket?"

"No," the Professor gently answered. "No, little Maxie" He smiled and gave the little boy a kiss on the tip of the nose, and that was no easy matter. "I was no pickpocket. But I caught many pickpockets."

"Oh!"

"And so I had to learn to do at least as much as they could."

"Yes, yes. Naturally. But for whom did you catch them?"

"For the police."

"Good heavens!"

"You're surprised, eh? When I was a young man I wanted to be a detective or a criminal investigator, and become very famous."

"Go on!" Maxie begged.

"Not now. Perhaps some other time. Today I'll tell you something about the display dummy we've bought."

"I'd almost forgotten him!"

"You'll have plenty of opportunities to remember him," the Professor said, "because we bought him on your account."

"On my account? What for?"

"Well, because you're so set on becoming an artiste."

The Little Man stared at him in surprise. "And we need the big dummy for that? Then what kind of artiste am I to be?"

"You're to be the conjurer's apprentice," said the conjurer.

∘7∘

On bakers' apprentices, butchers' apprentices, pineapple tarts, and
conjurers' apprentices · The doll is named Waldemar Blockhead · Hokus
outlines the course of instruction and the Little Man is shocked · The song of
"The Invisible Lieutenant"

So now the Little Man was a conjurer's apprentice, and naturally he
was very pleased. But he would have been even more pleased if he
had known what an apprentice conjurer really was. "I know what
a baker's apprentice is," he said. "A baker's apprentice must learn
the trade of a master baker. He must learn how to bake bread and
rolls and apple pie and pineapple tarts."

"Correct," the Professor said.

"And a butcher's apprentice must learn how to cut up meat and
to make all kinds of sausages and jellied meats."

"That's right."

"And if one has been a good apprentice, one is promoted to assistant. Someday will I perhaps be a conjurer's assistant?"

"That's not altogether unlikely."

"And if I . . ." Maxie began.

"Stop!" the Professor cried. "Do you want to be a master conjurer,
too?"

The Little Man shook his head. "The world would be an even
better place, dear Hokus, if I were to be treated, right now, to a
pineapple tart."

"You're a greedy little devil," the Professor said, but went to the telephone, ordered a pineapple tart and, for himself, a cognac. Then he sat down in a chintz-covered armchair and declared, "This is a tricky business. A baker's apprentice learns whatever the master baker can teach him. The plumber's apprentice learns whatever the master plumber can teach him."

"And the butcher's apprentice . . ."

"We'll leave him out of it."

"Why?" asked Maxie.

"Because if we don't, you'll get an appetite for sausage," Hokus answered. "Let's go no further than the plumbers!"

"All right. So I must learn from you whatever you can teach me," the Little Man said. "But that won't do at all! How on earth can I learn to swallow twenty big razor blades and then pull them, all strung on a thread, back out of my mouth? And after all, I can't produce a rabbit from a top hat! The sort of tiny rabbits I would need exist only in Lilliput, and Lilliput simply doesn't exist! And your playing cards and magic wand and bouquets of flowers and lighted cigarettes—all these are at least twenty times too big for me!"

The Professor nodded. "I've already told you this is a tricky business. All apprentices learn what their masters know: the baker's apprentice, the plumber's apprentice, the tailor's apprentice, the shoe-maker's apprentice . . ."

". . . the butcher's apprentice," Maxie added, giggling.

"Yes, he too!" Hokus agreed. "But you are the only apprentice in the world who has to learn what his master does not know."

"What do you mean? You can do everything!"

"Can I sleep in a matchbox? Can I fly around the room on Minna

45

the dove's back? Can I read books the size of postage stamps?"

"No. You're quite right. You can't."

"Or can I," went on the Professor, "peep out of my breast pocket? Can I climb on the curtain rod? Can I crawl through the keyhole?"

"No, you can't do those things, either. Gracious, there are things you *can't* do! Oh, that's a good one, Hokus!"

"Whether it's a good one or not," the Professor declared, "things are as they are. You are the conjurer's apprentice, I am the master, and with my help you shall learn a few things that I myself cannot do."

At this point they were interrupted. The waiter entered the room. He brought in the cognac and the pineapple tart. And very nearly knocked over the display dummy in the process. "Well, I never!" he cried. "Who on earth's this?"

"This is Winsome Waldemar," Hokus explained. "One of our distant relatives."

"A very pretty gentleman," the waiter declared, and winked at them gaily. "Has he a family name, too?"

"He's called Blockhead," the Little Man said, keeping an utterly straight face. "Waldemar Blockhead."

"You meet all sorts in these big hotels," the waiter said. Then he bowed to the display dummy, greeted him with, "A pleasant stay in Berlin, Herr Blockhead, sir!" and went out.

After the Professor had drunk his cognac and Maxie had demolished a tenth part of the pineapple tart with his tiny silver cake fork, the conjurer's apprentice began his lessons.

"You watched just now how I secretly appropriated a few objects belonging to the manager," the Professor said.

"I watched all right," the Little Man answered. "But I didn't *see*

47

anything. Not even the smart trick with the spectacles. I only noticed when you already had them on your own nose."

"Would you like to know how I learned that trick? I was once an apprentice myself, you know, and had to practice a long, long time."

"But how?"

"On a doll in a blue suit."

"Really? And did he look as handsome as Waldemar?"

"Waldemar is handsomer and blonder," the Professor had to admit. "But we won't allow ourselves to be distracted by his staggering good looks. Anyhow, when you've been climbing all over him day after day, perhaps you'll no longer find him nearly so handsome."

"What do I have to do?" Maxie asked, startled. "Climb all over him for hours and hours every day?"

"Yes, indeed, my boy. From shirt collar to the soles of his shoes, and from the soles of his shoes to his necktie. From top to bottom and from bottom to top, *into* all his pockets and *out* of all his pockets, nimble as a squirrel and soft as an ant in slippers—oh, you'll soon learn. You Pichelsteiners are, after all, celebrated gymnasts."

"And what, dear Hokus, is the point of my learning all this?"

"So that you can be a competent assistant to me in the circus. I shall be able to magic away many more things than before from the respected ladies and gentlemen whom I invite into the ring."

"Then you and I, no, then me and you, no, then *we'll* be a pair of thieves!"

"That's right."

"You'll be the robber chief. And what shall I be?"

"You'll be The Invisible Right-Hand Man."

The Little Man rubbed his hands. He often did that when he was

48

pleased. "That's like a cue for a song," he cried. And he began to sing right away, "The Invisible Right-Hand Man, ha-ha . . . I climb all over Waldemar."

"Go on."

"It's your turn now."

"All right, then," said the Professor, and sang, "I conjure with Professor Hokus . . . in the circus. . ."

"Hokus-Pokus!" yelled Maxie. "Now once more together! And very loud, both of us at the same time!"

The Professor raised his hands like the conductor of a choir, gave the sign to begin, and they sang with all their might:

> *The Invisible Right-Hand Man, ha-ha,*
> *I climb all over Waldemar.*
> *I conjure with Professor Hokus*
> *In the circus, Hokus-Pokus!*

The Little Man clapped excitedly. "Please, let's sing it again, three or four times at least! It's a wonderful song."

They sang it till the waiter knocked and inquired anxiously whether either of them or possibly both of them felt unwell.

"We're hale and hearty!" the Little Man cried.

"We're just being silly," the Professor added.

They sang the song to him slowly, and then the waiter sang it with them.

Then the maid came in. She was even more concerned about them than the waiter had been. But she was soon reassured. Finally the four of them were singing in chorus. It sounded like a community sing, but not as nice.

That evening, as he lay in his matchbox, Maxie yawned, stretched himself, and said, "So this was the first day of my apprenticeship."

"And the laziest," the Professor added. "Tomorrow morning we'll start working in earnest. Put the light out, Invisible Right-Hand Man!"

"Aye-aye, Robber Captain, sir!" Maxie switched the light off. The moon shone through the window. Winsome Waldemar was standing in the middle of the room, asleep on his feet. Minna and Emma, the two doves, were perched peacefully on his wooden head. It was not as comfortable as on the wardrobe, but it did make a change.

The Professor gave his first snore. The Little Man hummed softly to himself, "I conjure with Professor Hokus in the circus, Hokus-Pokus." And his eyes closed in sleep.

Hokus is an outsider · Maxie in the role of Maxie, the mountaineer ·
The mixed-up tail coats · The Three Marzipan Sisters · What is a trampolin?
Galoppinski conjures on horseback · Hokus von Pokus refuses to perform

They trained for several hours every morning. Afterwards the Little Man would take a bath in the soap dish. They trained in all the cities where the Stilke Circus played. When they were traveling, the display dummy would lie in the luggage rack of their train compartment, and they were careful to see that Waldemar did not fall down.

They did not travel with the numerous circus wagons which were coupled to a freight train: the caravans of the performers, the horse stalls and wild animal cages, the wagons carrying the big top, the wiring for the thousands of electric lights, the musical instruments, the heating equipment, the trapezes and tightropes, the posters and signboards, the costumes and carpets and seats and steps and pay boxes and animal attendants and cashiers and workmen and work-men's tools and the hay and straw.

Nor did they travel with Brausewetter, the ringmaster, with his top hat and wife, his four daughters and two sons and the sons-in-law and daughters-in-law and the seven grandchildren and the—now I really seem to have lost the thread—what was it I was trying to say, in fact?

Ah, yes, I remember. They did not travel with the circus, but took express trains. And they did not live in caravans, but in hotel rooms. The Professor was, as he said, a born outsider. "I like the circus very much," he said. "But only when it's filled with people. Apart from this, I like life and fine weather."

"And me!" Maxie cried as loudly as he could.

"I like *you*," said Hokus tenderly, "one-half inch more than fine weather."

For half a year now the Little Man had been clambering about Winsome Waldemar like a mountaineer in the Dolomites or in the Swiss Alps, except that he was not roped. It was dangerous work. For to him the tailor's dummy was as big as a skyscraper is to us.

Fortunately, the lad had a very good head for heights. For example, he would climb up the trousers, crawl under the jacket, run across the waistband, hoist himself hand over hand up the suspenders, jump across to the tie, climb high on the underside between the tie and the shirt as if in a rock "chimney" or *cravasse*, take a breather at

51

the knot, then swing himself onto the lapel of the jacket and, from the buttonhole, slide down into the breast pocket.

This was only one of his astonishing mountaineering feats. I won't describe all the others in detail. You know how it is—what I'm giving you is just a general idea. I won't explain in any greater detail the why and the wherefore of Maxie's daily climbs. For the time being, you must content yourselves with the fact that he himself knew what he was up to. But he talked about it to no one. And, of course, Winsome Waldemar also knew what Maxie was up to. But dolls and dummies know how to be silent as the grave.

Anyhow, the Professor was very satisfied with Maxie's progress. Sometimes he even called him "Maxie, the mountaineer." This was high praise which would make the Little Man's eyes sparkle with pride.

Despite this rapid progress, the period of apprenticeship would have lasted another three months, perhaps even four months, if one evening the two tail coats had not been mixed up. What two tail coats? The Professor's tail coat and the *haute école* rider Galoppinski's tail coat. It was a crazy business!

Brausewetter, the ringmaster, believes to this day that the whole thing was an accident. Yet nobody else in the Stilke Circus believed that: neither the fire-eaters, nor the imitation Chinese, nor the ice-cream sellers, nor the tightrope walkers. And the "Three Marzipan Sisters" didn't believe it, either. Rosa Marzipan, the prettiest of the three, insisted that it was an act of sheer spite. I suspect they were right. Jealousy obviously came into it. For Miss Rosa Marzipan turned all men's heads. Although that wasn't her intention at all.

As soon as the sisters, in their brief gauze skirts and flesh-tinted tights, tripped curtseying into the ring, the spectators would stamp and clap enthusiastically. It was impossible to imagine a more delicious spectacle. The girls looked nice enough to eat. No wonder they were called "The Marzipans!"

And then, when they had swung themselves onto the tightly stretched trampolin and leaped high, higher, and then yet higher, turned somersaults, hung horizontally in the air, or did breakneck jumps, the enthusiasm knew no bounds. One felt the three young ladies must be as light as ostrich feathers. Whereas in actuality the three of them together weighed a little over three hundred pounds!

Rosa Marzipan, the most beautiful, weighed about one hundred and twelve pounds and three ounces. That is not remarkably heavy. For example, I myself weigh about one hundred and fifty pounds, and that's only thirty-eight pounds more. All the same, no one would take it into his head to compare me with an ostrich feather. That sort of thing never happens to me. In this life, things never go as we want them to.

For those of you who do not know what a trampolin is, I should like to point out that it somewhat resembles a spring mattress. You, too, must certainly have often jumped about on your beds and been delighted by the bounciness of the mattress, the sudden weightlessness you felt, and the great leaps you could make. A trampolin is longer and broader than a mattress, and as tightly stretched as the skin on a drum or a tambourine.

Anyone who has learned to jump on it, and bounce higher and higher, can shoot into the air like an arrow, stay up for five or six seconds and, in that time, twist and tumble as if he weighed no more than a balloon. That's the sort of thing he can do. But only when he knows how to.

And, of course, he must also know how to fall right on the trampolin. For if he fell to one side, then he would break all his bones. Well, the Three Marzipan Sisters knew how to do all this. They had learned it as children from their parents, who had also been trampolinists in their day.

But let's get back to the mixed-up tail coats. It could not actually be pinned on him, but obviously one of the musical clowns, Fernando, had done it. In the ring, he would blow on a mouth organ as big as a plank, and then on another which was so tiny he swallowed it at every performance, and would go on playing it in his stomach. The spectators always thought that very funny. The clown himself, however, had long been a martyr to melancholia and bilious attacks because he was in love with Miss Rosa Marzipan and she would not so much as look at him. For *she* was in love with Professor Hokus von Pokus.

This made the clown mad with rage. And so one day, a quarter of an hour before the performance, he changed the two tail coats in the wardrobe! He hung the haute école rider's tail coat, with his top hat, on the Professor's hook. And he hung the Professor's magic tail coat and top hat on the haute école rider's hook. Then he slipped off on tiptoe.

When the Great Galoppinski pranced into the ring on his ebony steed, Nero, drew abruptly on the reins, rose up in the stirrups, and waved his top hat in salutation, Alba, the snow-white rabbit, popped out of the lining of the coat, flopped on the sand, and bewildered, began hopping around in circles! This made the horse shy and rise up on his hind legs. The Great Galoppinski patted his neck, trying to calm him down. Whereupon one dove, Minna, flew out of Galoppinski's left sleeve and fluttered all over the place trying to find the little table with her cage on it so that she could slip in through the open door. But the table and the cage had not yet been placed in the ring!

The stallion began to leap around, flinging out his hind legs. The band played the waltz from the operetta "Die Fledermaus," and hoped the horse would now perform his celebrated dance steps. However, dancing was the last thing in his mind: he raced across the ring as if he were pursued by a swarm of bees. The rider could barely keep him reined.

This made the audience in the front rows jump to its feet. Many people screamed in alarm. One lady fainted. The other dove, Emma, fluttered out of Galoppinski's right sleeve. He drew even more tightly on the reins. Then the stallion leaped with all four hooves off the ground and gave a mad whinny. The horseman reached for his whip to hit his unmanageable steed. But it was not his whip, but the magician's wand, which all of a sudden transformed itself into a gigantic bouquet of flowers! The horse angrily snatched the flowers out of his hand and tried to munch them. But they were made of colored paper, and he spat them out disgustedly.

By now the audience was in stitches. The rabbit was sitting up and begging. The doves were fluttering perplexedly around Galoppinski's top hat. The band was rendering the "Pomp and Circumstance" march. The rider gave his stallion the spurs in order to make him pull himself together and march in time to the music. But the black steed was not used to having the spurs stuck into his flanks in public. He lashed out with his hind legs and didn't stop shaking himself and kicking out in every direction, until Galoppinski, one of the best haute

école riders in the world, flew out of the saddle in one mighty arc
and landed in the sand!

Then the stallion, on thundering hooves, raced out of the ring and
back to his stall. The horseman got up and limped groaning after
him. The spectators were beside themselves, the whole two thousand
of them. The big top shuddered with their gales of laughter. It was
the first time they had seen a conjurer on horseback, especially one
who was finally unseated!

57

The ringmaster, Brausewetter, was standing at the entrance to the ring, shouting despairingly, "It's a catastrophe! It's a catastrophe!"

Galoppinski, who heard this as he hobbled past him, said, gnashing his teeth, "You call it a catastrophe? I call it a dirty trick! A filthy dirty trick! Who did such a thing to me? Let me get my hands on him! I'll feed him to the lions! Ow!" He held his back as he limped away.

The Professor dashed into the ring, grabbed the rabbit by the legs, enticed the two doves until they had settled on his outstretched hand, ran with them back to the pits, out of breath and nearly out of his mind. "I've been made to look an utter fool!" he complained. "If the President of the Magic Circle hears about this, I'll be brought before the Magicians' Union because I've damaged the conjurer's professional image!"

"But through absolutely no fault of your own!" Brausewetter said soothingly.

"I demand compensation!" Galoppinski roared. "In the first place, I was laughed at by two thousand spectators, and then I fell from my horse!"

"I should be going on in ten minutes," the Professor cried. "I wouldn't dream of it now! After the Great Galoppinski has made my tail coat a laughing stock? Never! And his old nag chewed up one of my most expensive bouquets!"

"He spat the rotten stuff out!" Galoppinski yelled, jumping with rage, then again crying, "Ow!"

"Please calm down, gentlemen," Brausewetter begged. "The show must go on! What's to be done now?"

"Under no circumstances shall I appear, not if you beg me on your bended knees," the Professor declared. "I shall take my animals, go back to my hotel, and drink an entire bottle of cognac!"

"Dear Hokus, don't do that," the Little Man called from his breast pocket. "I've a good idea. Hold me up to your ear. It's very important." And when Hokus held him up, Maxie began to murmur and whisper mysteriously.

The Professor listened in amazement, shook his head and said, "No. You must train for at least another three months. It would be premature."

But Maxie would not be silenced. "They've made a fool of you," he whispered, "and we are not going to tolerate that."

"No, Maxie. Not today!"

"Yes! Today!"

"It's too soon!"

"Please, please! Say yes! I'm asking it for my birthday. If you grant me this, I'll ask for nothing else! Not even the doll's drawing-room set of furniture!"

"But your birthday isn't for another six months yet!"

"That doesn't matter, Hokus."

At that moment the Professor felt a few very, very tiny tears on his big earlobe. He drew a deep breath and said, "Herr Brausewetter, I've considered the matter. I shall drink the cognac later. I shall appear! Announce my entry through the microphone! Do it yourself!"

"With the greatest pleasure!" the ringmaster cried, greatly relieved. "And what shall I tell the audience?"

"Tell my public that this evening, for the very first time, I shall perform with my conjurer's apprentice! And the number is called, "The Big Thief and The Little Man!"

·9·

---

*Ringmaster Brausewetter placates the audience · "The Big Thief and
The Little Man"—a premature premiere · Fat Herr Tynnee
and Dr. Hornbostel are robbed of everything · Brown and black bootlaces ·
Maxie waves to two thousand people*

Ringmaster Brausewetter kept his word. Barely had the "Whirl-winds," two famous roller skaters, disappeared from the ring, to great applause, than Brausewetter drew on his white kid gloves and signaled to the leader of the band. The orchestra played a fanfare.

The ringmaster strode with dignity to the microphone. There was silence under the big top. "Ladies and gentlemen," Herr Brausewetter said. "As you will have noticed in your program, the next act is Professor Hokus von Pokus. He is, if I may be allowed to express myself so, the Grand Master of all living conjurers. To praise him as he deserves would take all night. And no circus director has that much time."

"That's a real shame," a rowdy shouted from the back rows. But the audience hissed him down, and there was silence again. Only a horse whinnied, far away in the stables. Probably it was Nero being unsaddled and scolded by Galoppinski.

"Due to a mysterious *contretemps*," Herr Brausewetter went on with his speech, "*Maestro* Galoppinski seized a magician's wand instead of a whip. Whereupon he realized that conjuring and riding go together as little as . . . as steak and chocolate sauce or . . . or

60

as . . . as Cologne Cathedral and a railway terminal."

Some of the audience laughed.

"The outcome," the ringmaster declared, "is doubly distressing. For our Master Magician now absolutely refuses even to wave his magic wand again. I went down on my knees to him. I even offered him my stamp collection. It was all in vain. He is adamant."

The crowd grew restless. Some people stamped their feet and others booed. One man shouted, "I want my money back!"

Herr Brausewetter raised his hands protestingly. "Friends," he said. "The Professor will not perform his feats of magic, but—he *will* appear!"

The audience clapped.

"What he is about to show you today has never been done before in public. Even I myself, the guiding spirit of this circus, have not yet seen his performance. What is in store for you, for me, for all of us, is a WORLD PREMIERE!"

The audience clapped even more.

"I only know the act's name!" Ringmaster Brausewetter threw his white, kid-gloved hands high in the air and shouted as loud as he could, "The performance is entitled, "The Big Thief and The Little Man!"

Then he bowed elaborately and departed. The band played another fanfare. Everyone was waiting expectantly. And there was utter stillness.

"Well, this it it," the Professor said.

"It is indeed," Maxie in his breast pocket whispered. "Break a leg for luck, Hokus!"

"I've got my fingers crossed," the conjurer muttered, and slowly entered the ring. When he reached the center he bowed and said, smiling, "Ladies and gentlemen, today there will be no conjuring tricks. Today we shall simply rob you. Watch your pockets! Nothing and no one is safe from me and my young assistant."

"Where *is* this assistant of yours?" cried a fat man in the second row.

"He's here right now," the Professor answered.

"But I can't see him," the fat man called.

"Then please come a little closer!" Hokus kindly invited him.

The fat man, groaning, got up, came stomping into the ring, gave the Professor his hand, and said, "My name is Tynnee."

This made the audience laugh.

The fat man took a good look around and said, "I still can't see him."

The Professor went up close to the fat man, examined his eyes carefully, patted him on the shoulder, and said, "There's nothing wrong with your eyes, Herr Tynnee. They're perfectly all right. Nevertheless, my assistant is here. I give you my word of honor."

A gentleman in the first row cried, "It's absolutely impossible! I'll wager you twenty marks that you're on your own!"

"Only twenty marks?"

"Fifty marks!"

"Very well," Hokus said pleasantly. "Would you, too, be so kind as to step out here? We have plenty of room in the ring." He took Herr Tynnee's arm and waited smilingly for the gentleman in the first row who had wagered fifty marks. Herr Tynnee was smiling, too, although he had no idea why.

62

The gentleman strode up to them and introduced himself. "Dr. Hornbostel," he grunted abruptly. "Got the money with me." They shook hands with one another.

"Now, how about it?" the Professor asked. "Where's my assistant?"

"Plain silly," Dr. Hornbostel declared. "No such person. Not blind, am I? Want to double the stakes. Hundred marks?"

The Professor nodded. "Hundred marks. Just as you wish." He patted him on the chest. "Your wallet's fat enough. I can feel it through your jacket." Then he rubbed the material between his fingers, undid the middle button of Dr. Hornbostel's jacket, and said, "Best quality worsted, not an ounce of synthetic fiber in it, no creases, first class cut, expensive tailor."

"Right," the doctor said proudly, turning around.

"Wonderful!" Hokus said. "One moment, please! You've a piece of white lint hanging here. He picked off the thread and carefully smoothed the jacket.

Fat Herr Tynnee cleared his throat and said somewhat indignantly, "That's all very fine, Professor. Best quality worsted, expensive tailor and all that. But when does the robbery actually start?"

"In two minutes we shall begin, Herr Tynnee, sir. Not a second later. Kindly check the time by your wrist watch."

Fat Herr Tynnee glanced at his wrist and his face dropped. "It's gone!" he cried.

Hokus helped him to look for it. But the wrist watch was not to be found in any of the pockets and it was not on the other wrist. Nor was it on the ground. "This is very, very curious," the conjurer drawled. "*We* two wanted to rob *you* two in two minutes' time, and here's your wrist watch disappeared already!"

Then he looked the other gentleman straight in the eye. "Dr. Hornbostel," he said suspiciously, "I wouldn't like to suspect you, that goes without saying, but—did *you* perhaps, inadvertently, take Herr Tynnee's wrist watch?"

"Poppycock!" Dr. Hornbostel shouted angrily. "Wouldn't steal a thing, either inadvertently or as a joke! A highly respected lawyer like me simply cannot indulge in that kind of behavior!"

The spectators laughed heartily.

Hokus kept a straight face. "May I just make sure?" he asked politely. "You understand, of course, it's a pure formality."

"Don't mind," growled Dr. Hornbostel, and raised his arms. He looked as if he were being held up by gangsters.

Hokus swiftly searched all his pockets. Suddenly he gave a start. Then he pulled out something and held it up: a wrist watch!

"That's it!" cried fat Herr Tynnee, who snatched at it like a dog at a bone, strapped it on his wrist again and said, giving Hornbostel a sidelong look, "Well, sir, really! That's going too far!"

"Tell him it wasn't me!" the lawyer cried, offended. "I have a watch of my own!" He stretched his wrist out of his sleeve, made a stupid face, and exclaimed, "It's gone!"

The audience laughed and applauded loudly.

"A gold watch! Eight jewels! Real Swiss make!"

Hokus wagged his finger smilingly at Herr Tynnee and then went through all *his* pockets. Finally he fished a gold watch out of the right inside jacket pocket.

"That's it!" cried Hornbostel. "That's mine! Give it back!"

Hokus helped him strap on his gold watch with its eight jewels, and said, winking at the audience, "These two fine gentlemen have really been a lot of fun for me."

Then he turned to the two fine gentlemen. "Don't start quarreling with each other! Make up! Shake hands and be friends! That's right. Thank you very much!" He glanced at his own wrist watch. "In one minute I shall set to work with my apprentice. We'll rifle your pockets till you're scared stiff. But later, perhaps, we shall give some of your valuables back to you. It's well known that one does not thrive on ill-gotten gains."

"You and your non-existent conjurer's apprentice," Dr. Hornbostel cried. "Your hundred marks are as good as in my pocket!"

"All in good time, Herr Doctor," Hokus said. "The plundering will begin in a minute. Please look at the time, both of you! It's seven minutes past nine. Check your watches!"

Hornbostel and fat Herr Tynnee took a look at their wrists and cried out simultaneously, "Gone again! Both watches!" Indeed, both watches had vanished!

The audience roared its enthusiasm.

Then Hokus raised an arm to beg for silence. But, at that very moment, a little girl shouted, "Look, Mommy! The magic man's wearing three wrist watches!"

Everyone stared at the Professor. He himself gazed as if in astonishment at his wrist. Three wrist watches were flashing on his left wrist! The people laughed and yelled and clapped and stamped their feet with delight.

After the uproar had died down, Hokus politely returned the two watches and said, "Well, now, ladies and gentlemen, I really wanted to ask a third member of the audience to join me out here. As a sort of observer. But observation wouldn't have done much good after all. Do you know why?"

"Because you would still have gone on pinching like a thieving magpie!" laughingly shouted a lady who was thin as a rake.

"Wrong!" Hokus retorted. "He wouldn't have been able to observe anything because there's nothing left to steal. In fact, I've taken everything now." He patted his pockets and signaled to two uniformed attendants.

They fetched a table and set it in front of the Professor. "Now," he said to Dr. Hornbostel and Herr Tynnee. "Let's play Father Christmas. Turn around so that you can't watch me. And I'll put the presents on the table. It'll be a real Christmas treat, I promise you. However, you won't be receiving new presents. Only a few practical things which have belonged to you for a long time. I shall not give you anything you ask for, only the things you ask to have back."

"Pity," fat Herr Tynnee said. "I could have done with a new typewriter."

The Professor shook his head. "I'm sorry," he said. "We can't start asking for that sort of thing. Otherwise Dr. Hornbostel would probably wish for a Bechstein grand piano or a Wurlitzer organ. No, just kindly turn around and shut your eyes tight."

Neither of the men wanted to be thought a spoilsport. They turned their backs to the table and squeezed their eyes tight shut. The Professor himself made sure that neither of them was trying to peep.

Then he went back to the table and began to turn out his pockets until they were empty. There seemed no end to it, and for minutes on end the audience sat breathless. Meanwhile, the orchestra played an old, almost forgotten tune. It was called "The Policemen's Two-step," and was therefore admirably suited to the occasion.

Now I'm sure you remember how, when he was in Berlin, Hokus had robbed Hinkeldey, the hotel manager, and so perhaps you will not be as amazed as the two thousand people in the circus were. They went "Ah!" and "Ooh!" and shouted, "It's fantastic!" and "This beats everything!" One person even cried, "I'm going crazy!"

The simplest thing to do will be to list the objects the Professor unloaded. Here goes. He brought out of his pockets:

1 notebook, red leather

1 diary, blue linen

1 automatic pencil, silver

1 ball-point pen, black

1 fountain pen, black

1 wallet, snakeskin

1 checkbook, Bank of Commerce, blue

1 change purse, Russian leather, brown

1 bunch of keys

1 car key

1 box of cough drops

1 tiepin, gold with pearl

1 pair horn-rimmed glasses with case, buckskin, gray

1 passport, German

1 handkerchief, clean, white

1 cigarette case, silver or nickel-plated

1 package of cigarettes, filter tips

1 bill for coal, not yet paid

1 cigarette lighter, enameled

1 box of matches, half full

1 pair of cufflinks, moonstones

1 wedding ring, solid gold

1 ring, platinum setting, lapis lazuli

7 coins, total value 8 marks 10 pfennigs

The audience kept roaring its delight, and the two gentlemen with the tight-shut eyes shrank at every shout of triumph and every burst of laughter, as if they were receiving electric shocks. They patted and fingered all their pockets more and more desperately and, in the end, could hardly stand it any longer. For their pockets were as empty as the Gobi Desert.

Finally the Professor walked between them, laid his hands on their shoulders and said, like a kind uncle, "Dear boys, here are your presents!"

Then they turned around, dashed to the table, fell upon their possessions and, amid laughter and applause from two thousand people, hastily stuffed the things back into their jackets and trousers.

Because it seemed as if the spectators would never stop laughing, Hokus at last raised his hands, and silence reigned. The band, too, stopped playing. "I am glad you are laughing," he said. "But I hope it's not unkind laughter. Just remember that my tiny assistant and I could rob each one of you exactly as we have robbed these two nice gentlemen beside me."

"Tiny assistant," Dr. Hornbostel said scornfully. "Don't give me that again. And don't forget our wager!"

"We'll speak about that later," the Professor replied. "Anyhow, I thank you both for your active support." He shook hands with them, slapped them on the shoulders and said, "Good-by, and all the best to you on the long road of the future."

The pair turned to go. But Dr. Hornbostel had hardly taken one step before he stumbled and gazed in astonishment at his feet. He had lost a shoe and bent down to pick it up. Hokus came to his help and asked concernedly, "Have you hurt yourself?"

"No," the doctor growled, and examined the shoe in his hand. "But the lace is missing." He bent down to the shoe that was still on his other foot. "The other shoelace is missing, too!"

"Does this sort of thing often happen to you?" Hokus asked sympathetically. "Do you often go out without laces?"

The people began to giggle again.

"It's downright ridiculous," Hornbostel snarled. "I'm not crazy, you know."

"Fortunately, I am able to help you out," Hokus said. "I always carry spare shoelaces with me." He fished a pair of shoelaces out of his pocket. "Please take these."

"Unfortunately they won't do for me. I don't want brown. I need black ones."

"I've got black ones, too," Hokus said, and dipped into another pocket. "Here you are. What's wrong? Are they not black enough for you? I haven't any blacker than these."

"You—you villain!" cried Dr. Hornbostel. "These are my own!"

"Better than none at all," the Professor remarked. "And what shall I do with the brown ones? Perhaps Herr Tynnee can find some use for them?"

"Me?" the gentleman queried. "What for? I am certainly wearing brown shoes, but . . ." He took a cautious squint over his stomach at his brown shoes, size 13, and gave a shout. "Well, well," he cried, smiling. "My laces have disappeared, too! Hand them over, now. Otherwise I'll tumble over my feet on the way home! Thanks a lot, Mister Crookedfingers! Why don't you become a pickpocket? You would be a millionaire within a month."

"But I wouldn't be able to sleep in peace at night," the Professor answered. "Sleep is very important."

"Well, I'm the opposite," the fat man declared amiably. "*I could sleep in peace at last if only I had a million dollars!*"

Before he could continue this account of his black ambitions, he was interrupted by the sharp-eyed little girl whom we have already met. "Look, Mommy," the girl shouted irrepressibly. "That other man's just lost his tie!"

Two thousand people gazed at Dr. Hornbostel, the lawyer, who snatched suddenly at the collar of his shirt. And, indeed, the beautiful silk necktie had vanished! When the whole circus audience burst out laughing, Hornbostel became cross. "A joke's a joke!" he said glumly. "Please return my necktie immediately!"

"It's in your breast pocket, Dr. Hornbostel, sir," Hokus replied. Then he shook both the gentlemen's hands and thanked them heartily for their co-operation.

"You're welcome," fat Herr Tynnee answered. "But leave my hand alone, will you? Or you'll be snitching that, too!" He stomped back to his seat, taking cautious steps, so as not to lose his shoes. Halfway there he suddenly stopped and said, "What's happening to my pants?" He opened his jacket and shouted, horrified, "My suspenders! Where are my suspenders?"

"Take it easy!" Hokus called. "Could I inadvertently have . . ?"

He felt in his pockets and gave a start. "There does seem to be something here . . . one moment, Herr Tynnee, sir. I simply can't imagine how I . . . on the other hand . . . with my absent-minded ways . . ." And there he was, dangling a pair of braces in the air. "Why, here they are!"

The audience was in stitches. And when Doctor Hornbostel, tying his silk tie, nervously opened his jacket and felt for his braces, the people laughed all the more. But he still had them; he sighed with relief and mopped his brow. He was sweating with anxiety. Then he picked up the shoes he had tripped over and hobbled back to his seat in the front row.

The band played a fanfare. The trumpeters were laughing so much, they blew wrong notes. Fat Herr Tynnee was presented with his braces. And Professor Hokus von Pokus bowed elegantly. "The Little Man and my Humble Self," he proclaimed smiling, "give our thanks to the public for its exemplary attentiveness."

Then they all clapped and cried "Bravo!" and "Wonderful!" and "Fabulous!"

But Dr. Hornbostel had hardly sat down before he jumped up, gesticulating wildly, and shouted, "What about our bet? You owe me one hundred marks!"

The Professor gave a signal to Herr Brausewetter who was standing, beaming, at the side of the ring. The ringmaster passed on the signal. Then the circular cage that separated the audience from the ring when wild animal acts were being presented slowly rose out of its trap.

"Now I shall show you my conjurer's apprentice, The Little Man! You can convince yourselves that he really exists! The grille has been raised only to prevent you, in your enthusiasm, from trampling him and me to pieces!"

Then the Professor turned to Dr. Hornbostel, "There! You have lost your bet! You need not give me the one hundred marks. I have already extracted them from your wallet! And now I am returning the one hundred marks to you!"

Dr. Hornbostel counted the money in his wallet, whispered "That's right," and sank back into his seat.

Hokus took Maxie out of his breast pocket, held him up, and

shouted, "Allow me to introduce you all to The Little Man! Here he is!"

The spectators jumped up, lumbered down the steps, shoving and squeezing each other, and pressing their faces close to the grille.

"There he is," they cried.

"I can't see him!"

"Yes, he's there!"

"Where? Where?"

"On the Professor's palm."

"Ooh! Isn't he tiny!"

"Like a matchstick."

"You can hardly believe it!"

The Little Man laughed and waved to them.

∘ 10 ∘

The radio patrol car intervenes. The Little Man is promoted to conjurer's assistant · Two kinds of applause · Galoppinski needs a new whip · Rosa Marzipan throws her arms around the Professor's neck · Maxie sends his compliments

It was a tremendous triumph, and order was restored in the circus only after a radio patrol car with a wailing siren and a blue light on the roof had arrived on the scene. It had collected the Professor, the Little Man, the two doves and Alba, the rabbit, and taken them by devious routes to their hotel. The cars that tried to follow after them were thus shaken off.

A little later, Hokus and Maxie were sitting in the Red Salon at their hotel. They ordered a black coffee with cream and two spoons, took a deep breath, looked at one another, and smiled.

The headwaiter hung a sign saying "Please do not disturb!" on the doorknob before he gave the order for the coffee. He, too, had already heard of the sensational success.

"Well?" the Little Man modestly inquired. "Were you satisfied with me?"

The Professor nodded. "You did a very nice job. As you know, I really wanted to wait another few months."

"But we had to do something!" the Little Man cried. "We simply couldn't have just shrugged off the disgrace of your tail coat."

"What a dirty trick," the Professor growled, and banged his fist on the table. "Galoppinski was out of his mind. And the poor horse!"

"And our poor rabbit!" Maxie said. "I thought Alba would drop dead with fright any minute."

"Did you have a tough time?" the Professor asked, smiling.

"The suspenders were the worst. The left-hand front metal clip simply wouldn't come open. I broke off two fingernails. It's much easier with Winsome Waldemar."

"But then it went so much better with the shoelaces," the Professor said. "That was first-class work. And the trick with the necktie came off, too."

"Easy as pie," Maxie recalled. "The knot was quite loose. I was inside in a jiffy."

"Yes. Silk is pliable. That was lucky for us. Luck's part of the business."

The Little Man wrinkled his forehead. "I must ask you something, and you mustn't try to get out of it."

"All right. Shoot!"

"I would give anything to know."

"Know what?"

"Whether you now consider that one day I might become a real artiste."

"One day?" the Professor asked. "You're one already. This evening you passed your apprentice's test."

"Oh," whispered Maxie. That was all. He couldn't say another thing.

"Now you're my conjurer's assistant. All the way!"

"Are you sure the people didn't clap just because I am so little?"

"No, my boy. But, of course, that sort of thing plays its part. When Jumbo, the elephant, sits on a pedestal and raises his front legs, people clap. Why? Because he can do something and because he is so big. If he were just a big lump and hadn't learned to do anything, people would just as soon stay at home on the sofa. Do you see?"

"More or less."

"There are two kinds of applause," the Professor proceeded with his lecture. "Let's take another example. When the three Marzipan Sisters leap sixteen and one-half feet into the air from their trampolin, and turn somersaults, the audience applauds enthusiastically. Why? Because they can do something and because they look so pretty."

"Especially Miss Rosa," Maxie suggested out loud.

"If they were ugly, the three girls would not appeal half so much to the audience, even if they were able to jump six feet higher."

"Are there two kinds of applause for the clowns also?"

"Yes, there are! If they didn't have fat red noses and baggy pants and shoes like ducks' bills, their jokes wouldn't be half so comical. It's always like that."

"Is it the same for you, too?" the Little Man asked inquisitively. "You aren't as big as Jumbo and not as little as me. You haven't a red nose and you're not as beautiful as the Marzipan Sisters. What two kinds of applause do *you* have?"

The Professor laughed. "I don't know," he said finally.

"But *I* know!" the Little Man cried triumphantly. "In the first place, you're a terrific conjurer . . ."

"And in the second place?"

"Lift me up, and I'll whisper in your ear!"

The Professor lifted up the Little Man.

"In the second place," Maxie whispered, "in the second place you are the best person in the whole world."

At first there was a short silence. Then the Professor cleared his throat, and said, awkwardly, "Mmm . . . yes. Well, after all . . ."

Maxie heaved a sigh. "Do you know, sometimes I feel I should like to be the same size as normal people. At this very moment, for example."

"Why just now, eh?"

"Because then I would have really long arms, and could fling them around your neck."

"My dear boy," the Professor said.

Then, at last, the headwaiter brought the black coffee with two spoons. "The coffee-maker sends her best compliments and the little spoon as a present for the Little Man. It was the smallest spoon she could lay her hands on although she looked everywhere."

"And why is it a present for me?" Maxie asked, astonished.

The headwaiter gave a deep bow. "As a lasting memento of the day on which you became famous. The coffee-maker has scratched today's date on the spoon with a larding needle."

"With a larding needle?" echoed the Little Man.

"That's right," the headwaiter replied. "It's mostly used for larding roast hare and saddle of venison. The cook couldn't find anything sharper."

"Many, many thanks," Maxie said. "So does the coffee-maker think I am famous now?"

"Not only the coffee-maker thinks that," called a lady's voice. The exuberant tones belonged to Miss Rosa Marzipan. "Here I am!" the Marzipan girl declared. "The first reporters and photographers and radio interviewers are already lurking outside the front of the hotel. But the doorman is not letting them in."

"Good for him," the Professor grunted. "And how did he come to let *you* in?"

"I know exactly how she did it!" cried the Little Man, rubbing his hands. "She just looked at him and fluttered her eyelashes!"

"You've got it," said Miss Rosa. "He melted like chocolate ice cream on a radiator. The porter had to come and mop up the remains." Then she gave Maxie a little kiss, because he was so little, and an even smaller kiss to Hokus, because he was so big. "And now, I'm feeling hungry!" she briskly declared. "For saddle of venison," she continued. "A well-larded saddle of venison with potato croquettes and cranberry sauce. And you must try some, too."

Whereupon the headwaiter really got a move on.

After dinner she said, "This is the life, my friends. I enjoyed my meal, you are famous, and the Great Galoppinski needs a new riding whip."

"What for?" inquired Maxie.

"Because his old one's smashed to pieces," the young lady informed him. "It came into close contact with the clown, Fernando, for a few minutes. That was too much for the poor whip. And for Fernando, too, as a matter of fact."

"Because of the mixed-up tail coats?"

Rosa nodded. "That's right. The clown, though, wanted to embarrass not the rider and his horse, but a certain Professor Hokus."

"Hokus?" cried the Little Man in perplexity.

"Fernando is jealous because he thinks Hokus likes me."

"Well, he's right there!" Maxie cried.

Then the conjurer went as red as a blood orange and looked as if

80

he would like to vanish on the spot, if he had been able to—or to change himself into a toothbrush. But only absolutely genuine magicians can do that sort of thing.

Miss Rosa looked at him with sparkling eyes. "Is that true?" she asked, and slowly stood up. "Is that true?" she repeated menacingly.

"It's true," Hokus said gloomily, and gazed at the toes of his shoes as if he were seeing them for the first time.

"I could box your ears for you," she scolded him. "Why didn't you tell me, you wretch? Why didn't you fall on your knees before me long ago, you rogue? Why didn't you implore me to give you my marzipan hand and heart, you slacker?"

The Professor replied, "I'll give you a good spanking if you speak to me like that!"

Then she threw her arms in the air and cried ecstatically, "At last! The first words of love!" She threw her arms around his neck, making all the dishes rattle. Maxie clapped his hands. And Rosa Marzipan said, "I regret every day I didn't know about your love! We've lost a lot of time."

"Don't worry yourself about that," Hokus said. "You're still young, you know."

"That's so," she admitted. "And marzipan keeps fresh a long time."

After a few moments, someone nearby gave a discreet cough. It was the headwaiter. "Maxie sends you his compliments."

"But where's he gone?" the pair cried with one voice. They went as white as the tablecloth with shock.

"He's upstairs in your room, Professor. I took him up in the elevator. He's sitting in the flowerpot on the balcony looking at the view and he reports that he is highly satisfied."

"It's terrible," the Professor murmured when the headwaiter had departed. "We simply didn't notice that he left the room. I'm an unnatural father."

"It's high time there was someone to look after both of you!" Rosa declared. "Is the situation still vacant? I know of someone who would take it."

"I hope it's no one who goes bouncing about on a trampolin," he said.

She smiled. "I have no intention of spending the rest of my life turning somersaults in the air. I'm applying for the position, Herr Professor."

"You're engaged," was his answer.

∘ 11 ∘

Maxie in the pot of lilies of the valley · Frau Holzer gives a few sneezes · A specialist in Chronic Discontent · The Little Man grows and becomes a giant · He looks at himself in the mirror · The second magic potion · A completely normal boy

Meanwhile the Little Man was sitting on the balcony in a flower pot. It was a white earthenware pot. That morning, the hotel gardener had planted twenty lilies of the valley in it because he knew that they were Maxie's favorite flowers.

"Is there a poem about the scent of lilies of the valley?" the boy had inquired. But neither Hokus nor the gardener knew of one.

"Probably it would be as difficult to find as the quadruple somer-sault," Hokus had conjectured.

"But there's no such thing as the quadruple somersault!" the Little Man had shouted.

"I know," Hokus had replied. "That's the whole point."

Now as we have said, the Little Man was sitting in the flowerpot, leaning against one of the tender green stems, and gazing at the clusters of lily-of-the-valley blossoms above him. He was sniffing the fragrance that even poets cannot describe, and thinking about life. People do that sometimes. Even healthy boys. Even the Little Man.

He thought of his parents and of the Eiffel Tower, of Hokus and Miss Marzipan, of the mixed-up tail coats and Fernando, the Clown, of Galoppinski's broken whip and Herr Tynnee's suspenders, of the raucous circus and the gentle lilies of the valley and . . . and . . . and . . . and then he fell asleep and started dreaming.

In his dream, he was running, small as he was, down an endlessly long shopping street, feeling he would never be able to escape from all the boots and shoes. He was in mortal danger. The passers-by were in a such a hurry that they did not see him. They went striding past and over him, taking big steps, so that he had to keep jumping in wild zigzags over the pavement, terrified by their soles and heels. Sometimes he pressed himself against the wall of a house in order to catch his breath. Then he would run on. His heart was in his mouth.

If someone stamped on him, no one would notice it. And Hokus would search in vain for his Maxie. Perhaps a street cleaner might sweep him onto his shovel with the newspapers and cigarette ends and throw him into the trash can. What a deplorable and premature end for a young and promising artiste!

Look out! Another pair of heavy boots came clumping along. At the last minute the Little Man managed to jump clear! But, in doing so, he almost found himself underneath the sharp heel of a lady's shoe. In desperation, he leaped into the air and grabbed the hem of a coat. He clambered up the coat until he had reached the shoulder, and settled himself on a wide collar.

The collar belonged to a storm coat. And the storm coat belonged to a woman. She did not notice that she was no longer alone, and so Maxie was able to observe her undisturbed. She was an elderly lady. Her face looked good-natured. She was carrying a string bag and seemed to have bought all kinds of things. Often she would stop in front of a shop window examining the displays. Once she sneezed, and said aloud to herself, *"Gesundheit, Frau* Holzer!" Maxie very nearly burst out laughing at that.

The Little Man got bored while she was standing in front of a linen store, pricing the dish towels, hand towels, handkerchiefs, dust cloths, and napkins. To pass the time, he read the name plates on the house door next to the linen shop. First there was an establishment where children's dirty hands could be washed, then a convalescent home for limp gingerbread biscuits, and also a doctor's name plate which the boy stared at breathlessly. Could he believe his eyes? The name plate read:

85

Professor Wachsmuth
Doctor of Medicine
Specialist in chronic discontent
Free treatment for giants and dwarfs
Hours of consultation: any time you like
Second floor, on the left.

Just then, the lady sneezed again. "It's going to be fine weather," she said to herself. Again she caught her breath and went, "Hatchoo!"

Then the Little Man said, "Gesundheit, Frau Holzer!"

"Thank you kindly," she amiably replied. Then she started, turned in every direction, and asked, "Who was it wished me 'Gesundheit?'"

"Me," Maxie cheerfully cried. "But you can't see me, because I'm only two inches tall and sitting on your coat collar."

"Mind you don't fall down, then!" she said in a worried tone, and went close to the shop window to examine her reflection. "I think I can see you now. My dear young man, how tiny you are! A body doesn't see the likes of you every day! Won't you come home with me? Are you hungry? Are you tired? Have you a tummyache? Would you like me to put you to bed with a hot-water bottle?"

"No, thank you," Maxie replied. "It's awfully nice of you to worry but there's nothing wrong with me. However, I should be grateful if you would go next door and carry me up to the second floor and ring Dr. Wachsmuth's bell for me. Door bells are too high for me to reach."

"If that's all you want," Frau Holzer said stoutly. She marched into the entrance hall, stomped upstairs to the second floor, and pressed the bell on the left-hand door. She stood reading the sign.

86

"Whatever next?" she said. "A specialist in chronic discontent?" She laughed. "He wouldn't make much of a living out of *me*! As far as I'm concerned, the doctor . . ."

But before she could say just *what* the doctor might do as far as she was concerned, the door opened, and she caught sight of an old gentleman in a white doctor's coat and with an uncommonly rich growth of facial hair.

He looked Frau Holzer quickly up and down from top to toe, and shook his head. "I think you've come to the wrong door," he said in a sinister fashion. "You look so contented, you make all my corns ache."

She laughed in his face. "My! What a sourpuss *you* are," she exclaimed. "You should go and see a doctor, Doctor Wachsmuth, for example."

"It would be useless," he growled. "I can help everybody but myself."

"You doctors are all alike," Frau Holzer said, and was about to go on. But again she was overcome by a sneeze.

"Gesundheit, Frau Holzer!" the Little Man said.

At that, the doctor's eyes popped out of his head. "Well strike me pink," he grunted. "Here's a patient to my liking!" And in a trice he had seized Maxie and slammed the door in Frau Holzer's face.

"Why are you discontented?" the doctor asked when they were in his consultation room.

"I want to be bigger," was Maxie's reply.

"How big?"

"I don't know."

"Always the same story," the doctor growled. "Everyone knows what he *doesn't* want. But nobody knows what he *does* want." He took a number of brightly colored medicine bottles out of the glass cabinet and grabbed a spoon. "How about eight feet?" he drily suggested. "I can't make you any bigger than that, or you'll be bumping your head on the ceiling. Well? Out with it!"

"Eight feet?" The Little Man gazed up anxiously at the chandelier. "And what if . . . what if . . . I didn't like it afterwards?"

"Then I should give you an antidote, and you'll get smaller again."

"All right then," Maxie said in a trembling voice. "Let's try eight feet!"

The doctor hummed and hawed behind his luxurious beard, poured a few drops from a green bottle into the spoon, and commanded, "Mouth open, wide!"

The Little Man opened his mouth wide and felt a burning liquid
on his tongue.

"Get it down!"

The Little Man gulped down the green syrup. It flamed in his
throat and ran like wildfire down to his stomach.

Big-beard fixed his gleaming eyes upon the boy and muttered,
"It's taking immediate effect!" And he was right.

There was a sudden thundering in Maxie's ears. There was a
straining in his arms and legs. His ribs hurt. His hair and scalp ached.
His kneecaps creaked. He saw rainbow-bright circles spinning before
his eyes, with hundreds of silver and golden globes and stars dancing

among them. He could hardly recognize his own hands. They were growing and getting longer and broader. Could these be *his* hands?

Soon he vaguely realized that the glass cabinet was getting smaller, and the calendar on the wall was sinking lower and lower. Then there was a slight tinkling sound, because he had bumped the tip of his nose on the chandelier. And finally there was a jerk, as in an elevator that stops too suddenly!

The bright circles before his eyes were turning more slowly. The globes and stars stopped dancing. The thunder died away in his ears. His scalp no longer ached. His limbs no longer hurt.

And the doctor's voice was saying, satisfied, "Exactly eight feet."

But where on earth was Dr. Big-beard with his sour old face? Maxie looked all around for him. The curtain rod was right in front of his nose. The chandelier, that was still clinking and swaying a little, hung level with Maxie's chest. On top of the cabinet the dust lay inches thick. And dust lay also on the white, painted molding that bordered the yellow wallpaper half a yard below the ceiling. In the corner high above the door, a black spider was scrambling around its web. Maxie drew back in horror. In doing so, he knocked his hand against a high bookcase, and from the top shelf a book fell to the ground.

Doctor Big-beard laughed. It sounded like an old billy goat bleating. Then he cried mockingly, "Would you believe it? I changed him into a giant, and the giant's frightened by a spider!"

Maxie glared down furiously at the desk. "Why are you laughing at me?" asked the Little Man, who had all of a sudden grown so big. "After all, I have no experience in being a giant. Until just recently I was only two inches tall! Have *you* never shaken with fear?"

"No, never," said Big-beard. "Fear is something I have no use for. If a lion were to leap at me, I should change him, in mid-air, into a chaffinch or a brimstone butterfly."

"So you're not really a doctor?"

"No. But I'm not a conjurer like your Hokus, either."

"Then what *are* you?"

"I'm a real, honest-to-goodness magician."

"Phew!" gasped Maxie. He held on to the cabinet to control his trembling. And because the cabinet was unsteady, both the cabinet and Maxie shook.

"Sit on this chair and look at yourself in the mirror," the magician commanded. "You still don't know what you look like now."

Maxie sat down, blinked at the mirror, stared, and cried, "For heaven's sake! Is that *me*? Is that supposed to be *me*?" Horrified, he clapped his hands over his eyes.

"I think you look very nice," the magician remarked. "But we don't seem to have really hit upon what you yourself fancied."

Maxie shook his head as if demented, and muttered despairingly, "I think I'm hideous. Beside a freak like me, a giraffe is nothing!"

"Then what size would you prefer?" the magician asked. "This time, think more carefully!"

"I knew it right from the start," Maxie said contritely. "But I let my curiosity run away with me, and now I could kick myself."

"How big *do* you want to be?" Big-beard asked forthrightly. "Don't beat about the bush!"

"Oh," sighed Maxie. "Oh, Mister Magician—I'd like to be the same size as any normal boy of my age. No bigger, no smaller, no fatter, no thinner, and no freak like a rare stamp or a camel with three humps and no cheekier and no more timid and no more clever and . . ."

"That's enough of that," growled the magician, and grabbed a red bottle and the spoon. "So you want to be just an ordinary kid? Nothing easier. Open your mouth!"

Maxie, the eight-foot-tall giant, valiantly opened his mouth wide and swallowed the thick red syrup. He even licked the spoon. His head ached. His ribs and joints creaked and cracked. His heart pounded. The bright circles whirled before his eyes like fireworks.

And then there was silence.

"Look in the mirror!" the magician commanded.

Maxie hardly dared. He raised his eyelids only an eyelash width. But then he opened his eyes wide, jumped up from the chair, and threw up his arms, crying jubilantly, with all his might, "Yes! Yes! Yes! Yes!"

In the mirror, too, a boy had thrown up his arms. A nice-looking boy of twelve or thirteen. Maxie ran to the mirror, and beat with both hands against the glass, as if he wanted to embrace his reflection. "Is that me?" Maxie cried.

"That's you!" the magician croaked, and laughed. "That's Maxie Pichelsteiner, a completely normal boy of almost thirteen."

"Oh, I'm so happy!" Maxie said softly.

"I hope you'll stay that way," the doctor said. "And now see to it that your progress continues."

"How can I thank you?"

The magician stood up and pointed to the door. "Go your way, and do not thank me!"

·12·

"What a silly peacock!" · Extraordinary posters in the town ·
Ringmaster Brausewetter is suddenly called Brausepulver · Galoppinski is called
Traberewski · They make fun of him · Not even Hokus recognizes him ·
Max and Maxie · It was only a dream

Now at last he was just the same size as any ordinary boy. Other
children take such things for granted. But for him it was something
completely new. He was so proud of himself that he wished he could
have stopped every passer-by on the street and asked, "What do you
think of me now? Isn't it marvelous?"

Needless to say, he did not do such a thing. The good townsfolk
would simply have been very surprised and, at the most, might have
answered, "*What's* so marvelous? Boys of your size are two a penny."
They might even have become angry at him.

Many gazed at him in wonder even though he did not speak to
them. For he was radiant, as if he had just won a lottery. Besides, he
behaved in an extraordinary manner. Every so often he would
twitch or even jump to one side, as if he were afraid of being trampled
on. At such moments he must merely have forgotten that he was no
longer the Little Man. And yet now he was seeing faces and hats
and caps and not, as formerly, shoes and heels. But that is the way it
is with old habits. They are more difficult to shake off than the common cold.

There was something even stranger: he kept coming to a halt in front of shop windows. But *not* to look at the pretty, interesting displays. But because of the—as *he* thought—pretty, interesting boy reflected in the plate glass. He could hardly get his fill of gazing at himself.

On one of these occasions somebody behind him suddenly said, "What a silly peacock!"

This somebody was a boy of his own size, with straw-blond hair and a considerable gap between his two front teeth. "This the tenth shop window you've stopped to preen yourself in," the boy accused him. "I've never seen anything so sissy in all my life. Next thing you'll be giving yourself a kiss! Or proposing marriage to yourself."

Maxie certainly felt a bit put out by this. But, of course, the fellow could not know the circumstances. So Maxie replied calmly, "Leave me in peace."

However, the straw-blond boy had no such notions of calm and peace, but went on taunting Maxie. "You take steps just like a baby learning to walk! Come on, give me your little handie, in case you start falling on your little face," he said.

Maxie began to simmer with rage. "I'll give you my little handie all right," he cried. "Right on your fresh little turned-up nose."

"Oh, I'm so frightened!" the other mimicked. Then he began to laugh loudly at Maxie. "He walks like a tiny tot and thinks he can put me on my back! Ha ha ha!"

That was too much for Maxie. His anger boiled over like milk from a saucepan. He swung his fist back, punched, and the blond boy went sprawling on the pavement holding his lower jaw with his left hand. Maxie was very surprised. "I'm sorry," he said. "It's the first time I've ever knocked anyone down." Then he strolled on.

Apart from the mirror-like shopwindows, what began to interest him more and more every minute were the posters. Wherever he looked, he saw himself. Though the posters were not true to the normal-sized boy he had now become, they showed the Little Man, the conjurer's apprentice, the tiny assistant to the celebrated Professor Hokus von Pokus who was appearing within at Stilke's Circus and drawing such storms of applause. Maxie Pichelsteiner was everywhere to be seen, and the slogans seemed to be tumbling over each other in their eagerness to catch the eye. The advertisers had completely lost their heads.

In one of the advertisements he was leaning against a matchbox exactly the same size as himself, and the matchbox and Maxie were at least six feet high. The text of the advertisement ran:

The Little Man
The newly discovered Star of the Circus World
Sleeps only in matchboxes made by
Sirius Match, Ltd.

On another poster he was holding in both hands, a silvery, glittering, and much larger than life-sized electric shaver, and the big letters brazenly announced:

The Little Man
Shaves only with
WISKAWAY
Super 66

Maxie thought, "What impudence! When I'll have to wait at least another four years before I have the first hairs on my chin. Old Hokus'll be wondering what's up when he reads this rubbish." And the rest of the posters were no better. On one in which he was smoking a cigarette, there stood, in big, bold letters:

The Little Man
Prefers to smoke our health-giving
Manila Cigars. Highest Quality!
. . . and what do *you* smoke?
From now on, only Manila Cigars.
Highest Quality!

What queer people! The things they dreamed up to get rid of their stuff! Here they were trying to persuade the passers-by that the Little Man behaved like a grownup! When everyone knew he was still only a boy! Up there on the left had been pasted yet another poster with his face on it! He was waving in his hand a glass from which bubbles were sparkling, and the text read:

The Little Man,
Like every other Man of Taste,
Drinks on Festive Occasions
In the Company of Friends and Lovely Ladies,
The International Brand of Sparkling Champagne
FEMINA
Extra Dry

"What a lot of tripe," thought Maxie. Hokus was quite right when he used to say, "The advertising boys have nerves like old rope." Did the people who read this rubbish really rush into the shops and buy the shavers, cigars, and bottles of champagne they were so urgently recommended to purchase?

The boy was about to stroll on. But then his eye was caught by a smaller and more modest poster, one he might easily have overlooked. There was no gaudy picture on it. And no photograph. But the words he read went through him like an electric shock:

STILKE'S CIRCUS
Presents their first-rate show
Every Evening and Three Matinees

Special attraction
THE BIG THIEF AND THE LITTLE MAN
Sensation of the Year! ! !
Laughter and Amazement as never before!

Seats at box office and before performances

"Good heavens," thought Maxie. "Perhaps today's Wednesday or Saturday or Sunday. I must get to the afternoon performance! Hokus will be wondering where on earth I've gone." And he took to his heels there and then.

Ringmaster Brausewetter was sitting in the center of the ring, wearing his white gloves and black top hat, and reading a newspaper. He glanced up when Maxie came storming into the big top. "Where's the fire?" he asked.

"I beg you to excuse me," the boy stammered breathlessly. "But I don't know if it's Wednesday today."

The ringmaster raised his eyebrows.

"Or Saturday," the boy panted. "Or Sunday."

"Are you feeling quite all right?" the ringmaster asked irritably. "Here you come galloping into my circus and ask me if it's Wednesday! You might almost be charged with a breach of the peace." Then he bent his head again over his newspaper.

"But Herr Brausewetter . . ." Maxie was thunderstruck. Why was the ringmaster so unfriendly towards him, the new darling of the public?

"You don't even know my right name."

"Brausewetter."

"From the day I was born I've been called Brausepulver," the ringmaster declared vehemently. "Not Brausewasser and not Brausewetter but Brausepulver—and not Juckpulver and not Schlafpulver but . . . well, what?"

"Brausepulver," Maxie softly replied. He would have liked to sink through the ground. But then the haute école rider, Galoppinski, came into the ring and asked, "What are you getting so worked up about, Herr Brausepulver?"

"This young puppy's getting on my nerves," the ringmaster growled. "Comes running into the ring, asks me if it's Wednesday, and calls me Brausewetter!"

"Clear out, you!" the rider hissed at Maxie. "And double quick!"

"But Herr Galoppinski . . ." Maxie said, horrified.

"There you are!" the ringmaster cried, grabbing his black top hat with his white-gloved hands.

"My name is Traberewski and not Galoppinski," the rider yelled angrily.

"And today's Thursday, you blockhead," the ringmaster snarled. "Get yourself back home and do your homework."

"Well, I'm an artiste," Maxie shyly said.

"You don't say," cried the ringmaster. "We really needed that. What do you do then? Eh? Give us some idea."

"I can untie shoelaces," Maxie whispered.

Both men screamed at that, partly with amusement and partly with rage. Their faces went red as if they were going to have a fit. "That's going too far," the ringmaster roared.

And the rider shook his fists. "So he can untie shoelaces. We could do that from the age of three!"

The ringmaster was puffing and blowing like a walrus. "I'm going out of my mind," he groaned. "He can untie shoelaces. The boy's a genius."

"And I can undo suspenders," Maxie whispered, with tears in his voice.

"Now that's enough!" the ringmaster thundered. "That's the height of insolence."

"And I can untie neckties," Maxie went on softly and tearfully.

At that the rider jumped on him, seized his collar, and shook him backwards and forwards.

The ringmaster rose, moaning, "Spank him!" he cried. "And throw him out!"

"With the greatest pleasure," the haute école rider replied, and laid the boy in a workmanlike way across his knees. "Pity I haven't got my new whip with me," he added. Then he set to work.

"Help!" screamed Maxie, and the word echoed around the big top. "He-e-e-elp!"

At that moment Professor Hokus came into the tent from the stable and asked, "Who's making that awful fuss?"

"It's me, dear Hokus," the boy cried. "Please, please help me! These two don't know who I am!" He tore himself free, ran to the Professor, and repeated tearfully, "They don't know who I am!"

"Now calm down," the Professor admonished him. Then he looked closely at the boy and asked, "They don't know who you are?"

"No, Hokus."

"Who *are* you, then?" the Professor cautiously inquired. "I don't know who you are, either."

The boy felt as if an abyss were yawning at his feet. He felt dizzy. Everything started turning in circles. "Hokus doesn't know who I am," he whispered. "Not even Hokus knows who I am." Tears flowed down his cheeks.

It had grown very quiet. Even the ringmaster and Traberewski kept their mouths shut.

"But how should we know each other?" the Professor asked, at a loss.

"Because *I'm* your Maxie," sobbed the boy. He despairingly covered his face with his hands. "I'm Maxie Pichelsteiner! I am!"

"No! You're lying!" called a shrill boy's voice at that moment. "*I* am Maxie Pichelsteiner!"

The big boy dropped his hands and gaped, flabbergasted, at the

Professor's breast pocket. The Little Man was peeping out of the pocket and waving his arms wildly. "Take him away from me please! I do not like liars!"

"Dear Hokus!" the big boy cried. "Stay here! Stay with me! You're the only person I have in the world!"

"But Maxie," the Professor was saying. "Why are you weeping so dreadfully? Here I am beside you, and I shall always remain beside you! Did you have a bad dream?"

Maxie opened his eyes. Tears were still trickling between his eyelids. But he could see Hokus' concerned face bent above him. He smelt the scent of lily of the valley and realized that he was sitting in the flowerpot on the balcony of his hotel room. He had only been dreaming, and all was well again.

·13·

It was all a dream · A conversation before sleep · On the inventor of the zipper · What is "much"? · Maxie is still not the least bit tired · Mad lads and fast friends

"Was it really only a dream?" the Little Man asked, and sighed with relief. A millstone fell from his neck. "Oh, dear Hokus, what a good thing it is you can recognize me again."

"Do you mean I didn't know who you were? Now listen!"

"Because I was too big," Maxie declared. "As big as other boys of my age. And moreover, I was once more ensconced—as small as now and formerly—in your breast pocket."

"Maxie and Max at one and the same time? Heavens above!"

The Little Man couldn't help laughing. His throat did still hurt a little, but he was sure he would soon be cheerful again. "Take me in your hand, please," he said. "There I can feel how well you protect me."

"In any case it's getting too cold on the balcony," Hokus said, and lifted him out of the flowerpot. "You're now going to take a bath in the soap dish. Then you'll lie down in the matchbox. And you can tell me, before you go to sleep, what you dreamed about."

"Everything? The whole lot?"

"Certainly. The long and the short of it, and the short and the long of it. Dreams are deep things." Suddenly Hokus started. "Are you hungry? Or did you eat tripe and onions in your dream?"

"No," Maxie said. "It was a meatless dream. But all the same I don't feel hungry."

With the bedside lamp lit, Maxie related his dream. The long and the short of it, and the short and the long of it—about that nice Frau Holzer and her sneezes and about Professor Wachsmuth, who was a genuine magician and had changed him first into a giant and then into an ordinary schoolboy. He also told about his annoyance with the straw-blond boy. And about all the stupid posters. Then about the circus with Ringmaster Brausepulver and haute école equestrian, Traberewski. And finally about the ghastly shock he had when Hokus had come along with the Little Man sticking out of his breast pocket and had not recognized him, his own little Maxie.

Hokus was silent for a while. Then he cleared his throat and said, "There we have it. The dream has given it away. You would rather be a normal boy instead of the Little Man you are."

Maxie nodded in confusion. "Yes. That's what I've always wanted. Only I never told anyone. Not even you. Although I tell you every-thing else."

"And when you had grown up you suddenly became anxious and afraid."

"That's just how it was," Maxie said in a faint voice. "You once said that one must *be* something and *do* something. Well, I *was* nothing and could *do* nothing. When I told the ringmaster and Traberewski that I could undo shoelaces, they nearly died laughing."

"Because you were big! Anyone can undo shoelaces. It's only when the Little Man does it, that it becomes something they've never seen before. Only you and no one else can make the action *special*."

"It's not much," said Maxie.

"No," Hokus agreed. "It's not much. That's so. But it's much better than nothing. For who on earth can do 'much?' This actually happened: a man sat there for years in prison and invented the zipper. Today you find it on every suitcase and on many articles of clothing. That man discovered the zipper. Is that—'much?'"

Maxie listened attentively.

"Or someone runs the hundred yards one tenth of a second faster than any other sprinter on earth," Hokus went on, "and people are so excited they throw their hats into the stadium. Well, I keep my hat on my head. A new record was set up? All well and good. I'm pleased, too, and clap my hands. But is that—'much?'"

"Perhaps it's *not* much," the Little Man said. "But what's *more*? And above all, what is 'much?'"

"Preventing war," Hokus replied. "Conquering famine. Curing a disease that was considered to be incurable."

"Neither of us can do that sort of thing," Maxie said.

Hokus nodded. "Neither of us can do that sort of thing. Pity. Our tricks don't carry us very far. We can only do two things. We can astonish people and make them laugh. There's no cause for us to get delusions of grandeur. Nevertheless, tomorrow morning the papers will be falling over each other in their enthusiasm over our act."

"You really think so?"

"It'll be a sensation, my boy. There. And now we must sleep. Tomorrow is another day." Hokus laid his head on the pillow.

"I don't really feel tired at all," the Little Man declared.

"Herr Pichelsteiner, sir," the Professor said. "Would you be so very kind, and have the goodness to blow out the candle?"

Maxie tittered and switched the light off. "So now I'm little again," he murmured in the darkness. "Yet when you're near me, I feel all right."

"You must sleep!"

"Actually, we're both pretty mad," Maxie said. "Don't you think so?"

"Yes, yes," Hokus grunted. "Mad lads and fast friends. And now you must go to sleep."

"How do you mean, 'fast friends?' " the Little Man asked. "You don't look fast when you have your magic tail coat on."

"You must go to sleep," the Professor growled, and yawned so loudly, even the lilies of the valley on the balcony heard him.

"And how are things with you and the Marzipan girl?" Maxie asked softly.

"You must sl . . . ."

"I'm already asleep," the Little Man said hastily, and shut his eyes and his mouth. Whether he really did fall asleep at once I don't know. Firstly it was pitch-dark in the room. And secondly, I wasn't in the room myself.

· 14 ·

Fame in the morning · Telephone calls · The first visitor is Herr Brausewetter · Money isn't the main thing, but the most important secondary consideration · The rabbit in the wrong top hat · Headlines and rumors

The next day was a memorable one. Maxie woke up and found himself famous.

The head porter of the hotel, who in his forty-year career had acquired not only flat feet but also considerable experience, could be heard saying to the telephone operators as early as nine o'clock that morning, "This is no hollow celebrity, girls. This little fellow is going to be famous like the Leaning Tower of Pisa is famous. You mark my words!"

"Day and night!" *Fraulein* Arabella replied, and the other young ladies giggled and held their hands over the telephone mouthpieces.

Yet that day they didn't have much time for laughing. Calls never stopped coming into the switchboard. The whole world wanted to speak to the Little Man. Among the callers was an excited female. She wished to know whether the Little Man were already married.

"I saw him yesterday evening at the Circus," the lady said, "and I'm absolutely fascinated by him. Is he still available?"

"Unfortunately no," Fraulein Arabella answered. "Since the age of six he has been engaged to the Crown Princess of Australia. And she won't give him up."

"Why does he want to go down there among all those kangaroos?" the lady's voice said, taking on an irritable note. "I have a shop selling babies' and children's clothes. It would be much more suitable for for him. I beg of you, please connect me with his room!"

Fraulein Arabella shook her curly head. "Completely out of the question, madame! He cannot be disturbed. Please apply for an appointment by letter! And kindly do not forget to enclose your esteemed photograph. The young gentleman has a great eye for beauty."

Of course, not all the calls were as silly as this. But even reasonable telephone callers play havoc with the nerves and waste time when they come by the hundreds. The girls at the switchboard and the porter felt their heads were spinning.

Meanwhile, Hokus and Maxie were sitting on the balcony breakfasting quietly.

"You shouldn't lick the marmalade spoon," the Professor warned.

"Today it doesn't matter," Maxie claimed. "When one is as famous as I am, one may do such things."

"You have a somewhat extraordinary concept of the nature of

fame," Hokus replied. "It won't do at all."

The two doves were perched on the flowerbox. The rabbit was peeping out through the railing of the balcony. For the three animals this day so rich in glory was a day like any other.

The Little Man's eyes twinkled merrily. "Minna, Emma, and Alba," he counted. "All we need now is Rosa."

Then there came three knocks at the door, and their first visitor appeared. It was not Rosa Marzipan but the ringmaster, Herr Brausewetter. With one hand he swept off his top hat, with the other he held out the morning papers. "A sensational success," he boasted, and sank into a chair. "The press, although not present at the performance, has outdone itself. Curious sightseers are swarming outside the hotel. It has put years on the elevator boy. And the porter has lost his head and doesn't know where to find it."

Maxie laughed, and Hokus glanced over the newspapers with the first short reports about his own and Maxie's enormous triumph. "Things are moving," he said in a satisfied voice.

"And moving upwards, Herr Professor," Brausewetter added. "Pity we have to part." He gazed glumly at the floor.

"Wha-a-a-t?" the Little Man asked. "I don't understand."

Brausewetter wiped the top hat with his glove. "The Herr Professor must know what I mean . . . I think."

"I do," boomed Hokus, nodding.

"I did not have a wink of sleep last night," Brausewetter said, and put the top hat under his chair. "I've counted and counted. It's no use. Stilke's Circus is by no means a flea circus, but enjoys the gratifying respect of both the profession and the public. But since last evening you two have become world stars, and *that* I simply cannot afford."

Hokus replied, "But you don't know what salary we're asking."

"No. But I wasn't born yesterday. I know the sort of money you'll both be offered on all sides. I can't compete with that because I'm a reliable employer. Any other ringmaster perhaps would think like this: If I get that international number I'll be sold out every night, even if I have to turn the Bamboo Family out into the streets . . ."

"No!" cried Maxie.

"Or if I were to sell the elephants to a zoo . . ."

"No!" cried Maxie.

"Or if I were to give the fire-eaters and the Marzipan Sisters their notice . . ."

"No!" Maxie shrieked excitedly. "That you must never do!"

"I don't intend to do it," the ringmaster said with dignity, "and that is the very reason why we must part."

Hokus said, "Put your cards on the table! How much can you afford to pay us?"

"Four times what you're getting at present. But others will offer you ten times as much."

"No," Hokus replied. "Twenty times. In fact, I, too, was doing a bit of reckoning during the night. And you, dear Herr Ringmaster, can pay us more than four times as much, without pawning your top hat or elephants."

"How much?"

"Five times as much."

Ringmaster Brausewetter gave a painful smile. "But only if I give up smoking cigars."

"Your tobacco dealer would never believe you." Hokus said.

111

"He would be the last to," admitted Brausewetter, and gave a weary laugh.

"Have you understood everything, Maxie?" Hokus asked. "Put the marmalade spoon down before you reply!"

Maxie laid the spoon down. Then he said, "I have understood everything. We could earn elsewhere five times as much as with Herr Brausepulver, I mean Brausewetter. And even then, only if he gives up smoking."

"A smart boy," the ringmaster remarked.

"However," the Little Man went on, "how would it be if Stilke's Circus, now that we're so famous, raised its admission fees? Only a little bit? And if he were to pay that little extra to *us*?"

"A dangerous boy," the ringmaster declared, and began to sweat.

"At any rate it's not a bad idea," Hokus said. "But let's get to the main thing, boy! You and I are now partners, and your opinion from now on carries the same weight as my own."

"Wonderful!" cried the Little Man, and rubbed his hands with joy.

"What are we to do? Shall we stay with Herr Brausewetter? Or, for five times his money, shall we go to some other circus or to some celebrated variety hall like the *Lido* in Paris? Think it over carefully before you answer. A great deal of money hangs on our decision."

Maxie furrowed his brow. "Do you already know what you would like to do?"

"I do."

"I think I know, too," the Little Man declared. "I should like us to stay with Herr Brausewetter. It was he who engaged my parents, and he's always been good to me. Like an uncle."

"Bravo," said Hokus. "So we're agreed." He turned to the circus ringmaster. "Our decision is unanimous. We'll stay on with you."

"Oh," murmured Brausewetter. "I call that very noble of you." Deeply moved, he passed a hand across his eyes.

"We'll discuss the details this afternoon," Hokus said, smiling. "The business side of the matter, as you have noticed, is not the main thing for my partner and myself . . ."

"But?" Maxie asked inquisitively.

". . . but the most important secondary consideration," the senior partner went on.

The ringmaster bowed smartly. "Naturally, Herr Professor! Naturally! Well, now may I announce to the press and the broadcasting stations that you are to remain with me?"

"You may indeed, my friend," Hokus said, nodding.

Brausewetter was already on his feet. "Then I must get a move on!" He grabbed his top hat from under his chair and, in an excess of high spirits, set it at a jaunty angle on his head. But the top hat started wiggling from side to side as if possessed. "What's the matter with it?" he asked in bewilderment, and quickly took it off again.

113

Whereupon, with a big leap, the white rabbit jumped out! He was scared to death, and hopped as fast as he could across the room and into his basket.

"Look here, you!" Hokus wagged his finger at Herr Brausewetter. "That's unfair competition! Alba isn't having anything to do with strange top hats!"

The ringmaster laughed and wagged his own finger. "Tell that to your rabbit, not to me!" And already he was running as fast as his big paunch would let him, out of the room and out of the hotel in order to bring the editors, TV and radio stations, and news agencies the piping-hot news of the great good fortune that had befallen Stilke's Circus.

Only a few hours later, the readers of the city newspapers learned the great news. The central city editions even printed the news on the front page. The tall headlines ran:

> The Little Man Stays with Stilke's Artistes.
> Loyalty despite World Fame!
> Brausewetter beats all Competitors to it!
> Conjuring Professor and Conjurer's Apprentice
>   Renew Contract.

But the story under the headlines, and on the radio, too, was still quite sketchy, because no reporter had been at the circus the evening before. There were still no photographs in the newspapers. Even the lady announcer on TV had to console her viewers with promises of an appearance on that evening's show.

All the same, two thousand spectators had shared the experience and seen the tiny conjurer's apprentice with their own eyes, so the rumors running through the town had four thousand legs. Who ever would have thought that the clown, Fernando, would switch the two tail coats? And that Professor Hokus von Pokus would therefore decide to present the Little Man prematurely to the public? And because their success was still only by word of mouth, the whole thing was all the more exciting and thrilling and interesting.

That evening, before the second performance of the Little Man, over a hundred thousand people were swarming and pushing around the outside of the big top, trying to get in!

·15·

The second performance and the second sensation: Maxie becomes a flier ·
The Stilke Archives · A film offer from Hollywood · Exchange of letters with
the village of Pichelstein · A royal gift from the Kingdom of Breganzona

A hundred thousand people! Ninety-eight thousand too many! They besieged the box office for advance reservations. After a few hours there was not a single seat left for the entire duration of the visit, although Stilke's Circus still had another forty days to play in the city and, furthermore, the price of seats had been raised by one mark!

Three delivery trucks carried the money late at night to the safe-deposit vaults of a bank. Better safe than sorry, thought Herr Brausewetter.

The performance itself, the second performance that is, was once again a triumph for "The Big Thief and The Little Man." The people from the television studios had come with their cameras. Photographers were perched everywhere with their cameras and flash bulbs. Reporters and home and foreign affairs correspondents sat with wide-open eyes and their notebooks on their knees.

For the other performers, the evening, despite the sold-out house, was not one of unadulterated pleasure. For they all knew well enough that the impatient public and the press and guests of honor were waiting only for the appearance of Hokus and Maxie.

Yes, guests of honor were there, also. The mayor with a golden chain around his shoulders, his two deputy mayors, the city treasurer, the city councilors, the American Consul General, three bank directors, a host of film producers, managers and directors, and even the rector of the university, who hadn't been to a circus for the last forty years.

Professor Hokus brought two of these guests of honor into the ring and, at once, with the assistance of the Little Man, absolutely cleaned out their pockets: they were the mayor and the American Consul General!

Maxie ended by swiping the mayor's gold chain of office and the Consul General's suspenders. The two thousand spectators were vastly amused by that. And when the American almost lost his pants—who do you think laughed loudest and longest? The American himself! That made the audience more pleased than ever.

When the circular cage had been raised and Hokus had displayed his little collaborator to the astounded throng, he announced an additional sensation. "Ladies and gentlemen!" he called, "now The Little Man will fly up into the big top on the back of his friend,

Emma, the performing dove, and after a round trip high above our heads will return safe and sound to my outstretched hand!"

And so it happened. The band stopped playing. Not simply because it had been ordered to. They could not have brought forth a sound in any case.

The only creatures who showed not the least sign of fear during the adventurous flight were Emma and Maxie. With his right hand, Maxie lightly held the blue silk ribbon which Hokus had previously tied, with the greatest care, around the dove's neck.

Emma took off with the utmost smoothness, rose in a series of spirals right up into the big top, flew around the tent three times, and finally glided lower and lower, in elegant loops, like a little white glider, until she landed on the Professor's outstretched hand. His hand had never in all his life trembled so much. And the entire circus heaved a sigh of relief, like a giant awakening from a nightmare.

In the dressing room Hokus said, "I should never have allowed that flight. Never."

"It was wonderful!" cried Maxie. "And I am eternally grateful that you finally allowed me to make it."

The two doves sat up on top of the dressing-room mirror, caressing each other with their beaks and cooing.

The Little Man pointed at the doves. "Do you know what they're talking about? Emma has described our flight, and now Minna is jealous. But she has no need to be."

"Why not?"

"Because tomorrow it'll be Minna's turn," said Maxie.

It would naturally be quite impossible in these pages to give a complete report of their international success. But the circus press agent, with scrupulous care, collected and arranged all photographs, newspaper reports, interviews, and letters.

Anyone who is interested in such details must apply to the Stilke Archives. The press agent, an energetic and very helpful man, is called Kunibert Kleinschmidt, and is quite willing to give information to serious inquirers. (Enclose stamped, self-addressed envelope!)

So I shall pass over these trifles. It goes without saying that in the illustrated magazines there appeared large photographic essays, mostly very brightly colored. The French weekly, *Paris Match*, used Maxie, standing on Hokus' palm, as a colored cover picture. On television, millions of people could watch how Maxie secretly undid the mayor's shoelaces and drew them out of their eyelets. The American illustrated magazine, *Life*, offered the Little Man a hundred thousand dollars if he would write his memoirs and give them exclusive rights. An international doctors' delegation announced that it would visit Maxie to carry out, in the cause of science, extensive tests of the physical and mental capacities of the Little Man; then it would publish its report. An American film company was negotiating a contract for a wide-screen movie starring Maxie and the Professor in the leading roles. A match company put in a bid for a license to stick on all its boxes a label saying: "Let The Little Man Give You A Light."

Hokus accepted many of these offers. He declined many more quite flatly or, at any rate, provisionally.

"But the film in Hollywood—surely we could make that?" Maxie suggested.

The Professor shook his head. "There's time for that. Maybe later on. Take one thing at a time, nice and quiet."

But I must give a somewhat more detailed account of certain things. For example, the business of the letter from the village of Pichelstein which arrived one day. It read as follows:

Dear Max Pichelsteiner, sir:
Recently we were able to admire you on the television, which apparatus is the common property of the host of the Blue Goose Inn and thirty-eight other families. It was really exciting and we are right proud of you and of your artistry. We all knew your parents well before they left this village and you are their spit and image, a real chip off the old block. But even littler than they were, and almost more like them than they were themselves. We all cried out, he's a real Pichelsteiner, and drank to your health.

119

It was all very splendid and unforgettable.

We were able to follow you from the shoelaces right up into the roof of the big top, till we felt quite dizzy, and so we decided unanimously to elect you an honorary member of our Gymnastic Association, which you are as of now. We hope that this will afford you as much pleasure as it does us honor.

To our littlest man and greatest gymnast we send our heartiest congratulations as well as all the best to you and yours!

Ever sincerely,

Ferdinand Pichelsteiner

Chairman and Troupe Leader of the Pichelstein
Gymnastic Association. Founded 1872

Maxie was so pleased with the rather awkwardly written letter that he said to Rosa Marzipan, "Do you know what? I should like to answer this Ferdinand right away. May I dictate the letter to you while I'm sitting on the typewriter?"

The Marzipan sister, who lately had started coming often to the hotel room and helping Hokus with his correspondence, said, "O.K., young man," put a sheet of paper in the machine, put the Little Man on the carriage of the portable typewriter, and smiled. "I'm all ears!"

Then Maxie dictated his letter of thanks to Ferdinand Pichelsteiner, and while Rosa was typing he traveled on the carriage to the left until the little warning bell rang. Then she would shove the carriage, together with the Little Man, to the right and the trip would begin again.

Just as he was dictating, *"Your grateful Maxie Pichelsteiner, artiste,"* Hokus entered the room. He had been down in the hotel lobby discussing business with the lawyer from a Nuremberg toy factory and said, "Office closed, ladies and gentlemen! Coffee and apple pie on the way up!"

Rosa was about to release the paper when Maxie cried excitedly, "Please, wait a bit! I've forgotten something important!" And then he started dictating another sentence which had nothing at all to do with his honorary membership in the Gymnastic Association. It said:

```
Because all Pichelsteiners are very small,
it may well be that in Pichelstein there
is a girl of my own age and also of my own
size. If this were the case, I should be
overjoyed. Hokus, my best friend, would
certainly have nothing against it if she
were to come and visit us soon and stay as
long as possible with us.
```

"Naturally she could also bring her parents with her," Hokus said. And Maxie dictated:

```
She could also bring her parents with her.
We would send the traveling expenses at
once. And if you have no such tiny little
girl in Pichelstein, but have a boy, then
that would be almost as nice. Actually, I
would prefer a girl, because I'm a boy
myself. What I often miss is a friend of
my own size. . .
```

The Little Man held his head low while he dictated this phrase and traveled backwards and forwards on the carriage of the typewriter.

The Marzipan girl and Hokus exchanged a knowing look. "I'll tell you what," Rosa said to the little fellow. "You don't need to dictate the close of the letter to me with all the usual blah, I remain, sir, your devoted servant, and all that. I can do that on my own initiative."

Maxie nodded and murmured, "Thank you."

I must take this opportunity to mention yet another important letter. The sender was King Bileam of Breganzona. In his own kingdom, and also abroad, he has long been known as Bileam, the Nice. And everyone who knows him declares that "Nice" is not nearly good enough. He should really be called Bileam, the Nicest.

He wears a golden crown and a black hat, both at the same time.

The jewelled crown is stitched firmly to the brim of the hat, and it doesn't look at all bad. But enough about hat styles.

Anyhow, this King Bileam also sent a letter to Maxie. He, too, and his Queen and the Crown Prince and Princess had been enraptured by the television program. He hoped that Stilke's Circus would soon be having a holiday. Then the Little Man and his Professor absolutely must come at once to Breganzona to stay as royal guests in the King's palace. Princess Judith and Osram, the ten-year-old Crown Prince, could hardly bear to wait.

In the meantime, the two children had emptied their piggy banks and bought and dispatched a present for the Little Man, one which perhaps would give him pleasure.

Only two days later two sturdy packing cases arrived. "Royal Gift" was stamped on the cases, and that was no exaggeration. One case contained a complete, toy-sized, fully furnished residence: a living room, a bedroom, a kitchen with an electric stove, and a bathroom with cold and hot running water. Little lamps, water tanks, changeable batteries—everything was there, nothing had been forgotten—it was a little miracle of construction!

In the second case there was a big, low table on which the four rooms could be comfortably accommodated, one next to the other. During their unpacking, Rosa and Hokus had very nearly failed to notice a cellophane bag. They had almost thrown it away with the packing material. That would have been a pity. For in the bag there was a narrow silken rope ladder which could be hooked onto the edge of the table and up whose rungs Maxie could clamber to reach his comfortable private dwelling.

This he did almost as soon as the residence had been set up on the table. He felt happy as he strolled through the rooms, switching on the lights. Then, on the cooking stove, he tried frying a morsel of steak, which the waiter had brought, putting a knob of butter and some chopped onion in the small frying pan. They all had a taste, even the waiter, and found the sample excellent.

Maxie himself could not express any opinion on its excellence. There was nothing left over for him to taste.

After the performance at the circus, he bathed in his own bathtub and told Hokus, who was looking on in amusement, "Of course, this is something quite different from that silly soap dish."

Then he lay down in the heavenly soft bed in his own bedroom, stretched luxuriously, and murmured, "Of course, this is something quite different from that old matchbox."

But the next morning, there he was lying in the old matchbox on the old bedside table.

"Well, now," Hokus said, "what's happened?"

The Little Man grinned in embarrassment. "I changed around in the middle of the night."

"But why?"

"The old matchbox is of course something quite different," Maxie explained.

·16·

The Little Man in his own home · And fame is tiring · The second letter from Pichelstein · Nuremberg toy · A song becomes popular · Hokus makes the frightful discovery: Maxie has vanished without a trace!

The present from King Bileam and his two offspring provided once more, in that telling phrase, grist for the photographer's mill. They thronged into the hotel room with their cameras, snapped the contents of the little dwelling, and bestowed upon the world a new series of pictures with terrific captions: "The Little Man in apron and chef's cap at his own stove," "The Little Man taking a nap in his new rocking chair," "The Little Man in front of the bookcase with his miniature books," "The Little Man in the heavenly bed from Breganzona," "The Little Man for the first time in a bathtub," "The Little Man shows his rooms to the doves, Minna and Emma," and so on, as if it would never end.

When all the hard-boiled newsmen with their cameras and flash bulbs had finally gone, Maxie angrily tore his hair and shouted three times, "Why aren't I 'The Invisible Right-Hand Man?'"

"Fame is a strain," Hokus remarked. "That's the way it is. Anyhow, we'll stick the photos in an album and send them to Breganzona. The king and the king's children will certainly be pleased with them."

"Let's do that," said the Little Man. "But we must decline the invitation for the time being. Fame is a strain." Then he slipped into his track suit and for an hour clambered all over Winsome Waldemar. After that he lay down in the matchbox, gave a mighty yawn, and murmured before falling asleep, "Fame is tiring."

A few days later there came a second letter from Pichelstein. Ferdinand Pichelsteiner, chairman of the Gymnastic Association, wrote to the honorable honorary member that the village could provide neither a girl nor a boy of Maxie's size. He wrote:

> *From time to time of course young married couples have set out into the wide, wide world. But, what became of most of them was something which unfortunately we have never heard. They haven't even let us know whether they are still alive or dead. Not to mention what has become of them in the world. We just don't know.*
>
> *If we should hear of anything likely, we'll let you know at once. This I solemnly promise you: you can rely on the gymnast's oath. I am fifty years old and still active. Especially on the high parallel bars.*
>
> *Your faithful namesake,*
Ferdinand Pichelsteiner

Hokus slowly folded the letter and said, "Don't take it too hard, boy."

"Oh, dear!" said Maxie. He was sitting in his tiny drawing room on the green sofa and swinging his legs. "Naturally it would have been lovely. All the more so now that I have a house. The girl could have slept in the bed, since I like it much better in the matchbox."

"But the new bed is much more comfortable."

"I know, I know," Maxie said. "But it's too far away from your bed for my liking."

Now have I already mentioned the lawyer with whom Hokus had spoken in the hotel lobby? He had come on business from a firm of Nuremberg toymakers. They had discussed and negotiated. They had come to an agreement and signed contracts. And then one day it finally happened: the Nuremberg factory sent a parcel containing ten matchboxes.

Ten matchboxes? Yes. Full of matches? No. But in each box there lay, on white cotton wool, a Little Man! Ten Little Men, as like our Maxie as peas in a pod! In ten suits of pyjamas, striped gray and blue, exactly like the sleep suit Maxie liked more than any other. The ten Maxies had moveable limbs. One could take them out of the matchboxes and stand them up. One could put them back again. One could lay them down, as if they were sleeping.

In short, it was a new toy that very soon afterwards was being sold in all lands and in all kinds of shops as well as at the circus, and was very successful. Not only for the factory, but also for "The Big Thief and The Little Man," since they received a percentage of all sales. That was why Hokus had bargained with the lawyer from Nuremberg in the hotel lobby. For Professor Hokus von Pokus was not only a celebrated conjurer, but also a very shrewd businessman.

I would not have said so much about the new toy if these confounded Nuremberg matchboxes did not have an important part to play in the next chapter. But please be patient a little longer. For . . .

For I should like, before we come to that, to tell you about a song that came out around the same time and very quickly became popular. It could also be bought as a record. It was sung on the radio, and people danced to it in the dance halls. The music was composed by Romano Korngiebel, conductor of the circus band. I do not know who was responsible for the lyrics. The title was:

THE SONG OF THE LITTLE MAN

I've even remembered a few verses. It began like this:

> *What's all the fuss about?*
> *The folk they stand and chatter.*
> *They ask each other whether*
> *They've seen the Little Man.*
> *They inquired of ten policemen*
> *Who really should have known,*
> *But didn't know a thing about*
> *The Little Man.*

After this verse, all kinds of people were asked if they had seen the Little Man. Until it got to this:

> *A fat woman shouted then,*
> *I know him well and good!*
> *He sleeps till half-past-ten*
> *In a matchbox made of wood.*
> *He's two inches in weight*

He's two ounces in height
And he often corresponds
With nice King Bileam.
The boy even
Thieves like a raven.
Yet he returns it all
To the owners, big and small . . ."

Here my memory loses the thread again. I can only remember the ending. Here we are told that anyone who wanted to see the Little Man would have to jolly well hurry up, because lately he had visibly begun to get smaller:

After Tuesday you won't see him any more.
He's getting smaller day by day.
On Monday there's still a chance.
But on Tuesday, Tuesday,
Tuesday . . . He'll have vanished away.

"On Tuesday he'll have vanished away!" This last line of the song was to become very significant. And indeed, significant in such an awful way that I can hardly bring myself to write it down.

Please don't be too alarmed! I can neither change nor conceal what happened. But how on earth shall I begin? Hold tight to your chair or the table top or your pillow! And don't tremble too much! You must promise me. Otherwise I would rather tell you nothing at all. All right? Not trembling too much? Here goes:

On Tuesday he'd vanished!

What?

Maxie had vanished!

He had disappeared from the face of the earth.

When Hokus entered the hotel room, Emma and Minna were hopping about distractedly on top of the wardrobe. Hokus asked Maxie, who was lying peacefully in his matchbox, "What on earth's the matter with the doves? Have you any idea?"

As the Little Man did not answer, the Professor said, "Hey, there, my young friend, have you lost your tongue?"

Silence again.

"Maxie Pichelsteiner!" Hokus shouted. "I'm speaking to you! If you don't answer me at once I'll . . . I'll . . ."

Not a word. Not a titter. Nothing.

Fear shot through Hokus as swift and sharp as a flash of lightning. He bent over the matchbox, then ran and flung open the room door, dashed out into the corridor, and yelled, "Maxie, where are you? Maxie!"

No reply. Dead stillness.

Hokus ran back into the room, snatched the telephone from its rest, and had to sit down, so weak did he feel. "Switchboard?" he cried. "Alert the police at once! Maxie has disappeared! The hotel manager is responsible for not letting anyone leave the hotel. No guest and no employee must leave! Don't ask questions! Do as I tell you!"

He slammed the receiver down, jumped up, went to the bedside table, and hurled the matchbox together with Maxie against the wall with all his strength!

For it wasn't Maxie at all, but one of the confounded Nuremberg toy matchboxes with a little doll inside wearing gray and blue striped pyjamas.

·17·

Excitement in the hotel · The false room waiter · It smells of a hospital ·
Detective Steinbeiss enters the scene · Maxie's awakening · An important
announcement on the radio · Otto and Bernard · The Little Man wants a taxi,
and Otto gets an attack of the giggles

It could only be a kidnapping case. But who had stolen Maxie? And why? And why had he done it in such a carefully planned way? For he had, after all, exchanged a doll for the Little Man, so that the abduction would not be discovered immediately!

One of the room maids had seen a waiter coming out of the room. No, she had never seen him before, but she thought he must have been called from another floor to help out. But neither the head floor waiter nor the restaurant had given such orders.

"So presumably he was not a waiter," the hotel manager said, "but a crook who had put on a white jacket."

The room maid asked, "But then why didn't the little fellow cry for help? I'd have heard him, sure as sure."

"They drugged him," Hokus explained. "Don't you smell anything?"

The other two raised their noses in the air and sniffed. The manager nodded, "You're right, Herr Professor. It smells of a hospital. Chloroform?"

"Ether," Hokus answered. He was in despair.

Detective Steinbeiss, too, who was in charge of the investigation, was unable to offer any consolation. When he entered the room he was holding a waiter's white jacket. "We found it in one of the trash cans standing in the yard. The man obviously escaped by the tradesman's entrance before the hotel was closed off."

"Anything else?" the manager asked. "Any fingerprints?"

"Nothing," replied Steinbeiss. "I've sent my men away. For the last hour they've been searching the matchboxes of everyone who wanted to leave the hotel. It was useless. There was no Little Man in any of the boxes. They all contained matches."

"The airport, the railway stations, the main roads out of town?" Hokus queried.

"We're doing all we can," Steinbeiss answered. "I haven't much hope. Easier to find the proverbial needle in a haystack."

"The radio?"

"Is broadcasting our special announcement every half hour. Also the news of the reward of twenty thousand marks which you have offered is being regularly relayed."

Hokus went out on the balcony and gazed up at the sky. He could not discover his Maxie there, either. After a while he turned and said, "I should like to increase the amount of the reward. Anyone who gives us final proof of where Maxie is will receive fifty thousand marks."

"The radio stations will be informed of it immediately," the detective said. "Perhaps it'll be of some help. If we're dealing with a large gang, one of the kidnappers might well sing. Fifty thousand marks is not chicken feed."

"Why would he *sing?*" the room maid asked. "Sing for fifty thousand marks? What use would that be to us?"

The detective made an impatient gesture. " 'Sing' is a professional term and means more or less to betray."

"The whole thing's beyond me," the manager said. "For heaven's sake, what would anyone want to do with a kidnapped boy who's only two inches tall and as famous as Chaplin and Churchill? They can't sell him to another circus. They can't even exhibit him privately. Not for one minute! The police would be there in a shake of a cow's tail."

The room maid put on a conspiratorial expression. "Perhaps they want to extort money from the Professor," she whispered. "Perhaps they'll only give Maxie back after the Professor's placed a parcel containing a great big sum of money in a hollow tree under cover of night."

The manager shrugged his shoulders. "But then the gang would have to telephone or send an express letter!"

"Or maybe it's simply the work of a few maniacs. There's plenty of them about. If so, we're completely helpless."

Who knows what else she might have come out with had not Rosa Marzipan dashed into the room and, sobbing, flung her arms around the Professor's neck. "My poor Hokus!"

Behind her came, with measured tread, Herr Ringmaster Brausewetter. He was carrying his top hat, and on his hands he wore, as always except when in bed, kid gloves. Today their color was a medium gray. He put on black kid gloves only for funerals and white ones only for happy and festive occasions. He was most particular about the color of his kid gloves.

"My dear Herr Professor," he cried, "we are all deeply distressed, and I wish to convey to you the sympathy of all your colleagues. At the general meeting of employees ten minutes ago, we passed the unanimous resolution not to give any more performances until the Little Man is once more in our midst. Until then, Stilke's Circus will remain closed."

"What's the use of that?" the room maid asked.

Brausewetter gave her a sharp look. "It's primarily a gesture of friendship and solidarity, my dear!"

"And it may even be of some help," Steinbeiss declared. "It will increase the alertness of the general public."

Rosa Marzipan shook her head. "There's only one person who can help us in this."

The manager opened his eyes wide. "Who's that?" he asked.

"You're quite right," Hokus told Rosa. "He's our only hope."

"But *who?*" repeated the manager.

Miss Marzipan said simply, "Maxie himself!"

When the Little Man came to his senses, his head was throbbing. Yes, he was still lying in his matchbox. But he did not recognize the light hanging from the ceiling. Where on earth was he?

Dance music was coming from a radio. Blue cigarette smoke was swimming on the air. And suddenly a surly man's voice said, "Otto, see if the dwarf's awake yet." Because nobody moved, the voice went on angrily, "Would you rather I sent you a written invitation?"

"You're too hasty, that's what's the matter with you," another voice answered good naturedly. "It can't be good for your health, Bernard. Remember your heart!" But then a chair was scraped back. Someone stood up heavily and slowly came closer. Obviously it was the man called Otto.

Maxie shut his eyes, breathed regularly, and felt someone bending over him. Otto was breathing hard, and he smelled like a cigarette factory standing next to a spirits factory. "The little fellow's still asleep," said Otto's voice. "Let's hope you didn't give him too big a whiff of ether, Bernard m'dear. Otherwise *Señor* Lopez will have one of his bandits give your skull a nice going over!"

"Shut your trap!" Bernard's voice growled. "I carried out the deal as planned . . ."

At that moment the dance music broke off on the radio, and a third voice announced, "Attention! Stand by! We're going to repeat an important message!"

"If it's not from the cops, I'll eat my hat . . ." Otto began.

"Quiet!" hissed Bernard.

Maxie held his breath and listened carefully.

"As we have already announced," the radio announcer said, "this morning the Little Man, well known to all of you, was kidnapped from his hotel room. The kidnapper was disguised as a floor waiter. The white jacket used by him has been identified. The Criminal Investigation Department is asking the public for their strongest support. Professor Hokus von Pokus has raised the reward he is offering to fifty thousand marks. Any relevant information should be passed on to this radio station or directly to Detective Inspector Steinbeiss. Stilke's Circus has announced that all performances are canceled until further notice. End of the message!" Then the dance music started again.

After a pause, Otto could be heard saying in awestruck tones, "By gum! This Hokuspokus is really making a splash! Fifty thousand marks? I call that easy money! Don't you think so, Bernard? What about it?"

"You always were and always will be a thorough blockhead," Bernard's voice growled. "Fifty thousand? You don't give up a permanent position for that kind of money."

"All right," Otto murmured. "It was only an idea."

"You're not the one who has ideas," Bernard answered roughly. "Leave that to me, got it? Right. Now I'm going to telephone." A chair was pushed back violently. "And keep a good watch on the dwarf while I'm out!"

When the room door had closed, Maxie ventured to open his eyes a fraction. At an untidy table squatted a huge, bald-headed man, holding up an empty bottle to the light. So that was Otto!

"Drink's bad. No drink's even worse," Otto muttered to himself, and put down the bottle so hard that the table shook.

"Now or never!" thought Maxie, and pretended to wake up. He gave such a jerk that the matchbox almost overturned. Then he shouted, "Help! Where am I?" Then he gazed about him in bewilderment, whimpered, and put both hands over his mouth. It was a virtuoso piece of acting.

Otto, taken completely by surprise, got an extraordinary shock. He leaped from his chair and hissed angrily, "Will you shut your trap, you little monkey?"

Maxie yelled, "I want to know where I am! How dare you talk to me like that! And who are you anyhow? Help! Hokus! He-e-e-lp!" He hoped someone in the vicinity might hear him. But nothing stirred. No one had heard him, apart from this besotted, bald man called Otto.

"If you start bellowing again, I'll put a length of tape over your trap," Otto said grimly.

"I don't care for your tone," Maxie retorted. "Kindly call me a taxi."

Whereupon Otto was overcome with a fit of the giggles. It was, to be more precise, a mixture of laughter, coughing, sneezing, and wheezing. It seemed likely that he might explode at any minute. But he did not explode. When he had finally gained control over himself again, he wiped the tears from his eyes and gasped, "A taxi? If that's all you need, sir! Bernard's just gone out to inquire about a plane!"

·18·

Who bought the waiter's white jacket? · Great excitement at "The Golden Ham" · A report in the evening newspaper · Bald Otto bellows · The empty house · Bernard is the more dangerous · At night, Maxie explores the horrible room

The white jacket had been bought in a speciality shop for professional uniforms two days before the Little Man was kidnapped.

This is what the police finally established. At this shop one could buy butchers' aprons, chefs' hats, doctors' smocks, nurses' caps, canal workers' overalls, divers' helmets, sleeve protectors for bookkeepers, kneepads for parquet floor layers and mosaic tilers—in short, it was a big, gay shop. And the assistants had been extremely obliging to the gentlemen from the Criminal Investigation Bureau. But nobody could now remember who had bought the waiter's white jacket nor how he had looked.

Rosa Marzipan had persuaded Hokus to go out to a restaurant with her. "You really must have something to eat," she had declared. "You can't go on sitting in your hotel room staring at the walls. That doesn't get you anywhere at all. And you'll fall ill yourself in the end."

So now they were sitting in "The Golden Ham" as the inn was called, and Hokus was staring, not at the wall, but at his plate. He could not swallow a bite nor could he utter a word. It had been like this for the past day and a half, and Miss Marzipan was becoming seriously worried. He had sipped a cup of consommé. That was all.

In order to console him, she said, "Maxie will be back again tomorrow or the day after tomorrow at the latest. He is much too smart and clever to allow himself to be shut up for longer than that. Wild horses wouldn't stop him from escaping!"

"Unfortunately it's not horses that are stopping him," Hokus retorted. "It's crooks. Who knows what they have done to the little fellow." He sighed. Then he shook his head. "Not even the higher reward seems to tempt them! And I was hoping that it would make them telephone me immediately."

"They're afraid of the police."

"For Maxie's sake, I would not give the crooks away," Hokus murmured, and stared down at his plate. Rosa Marzipan, too, had no appetite. But she ate a few bites, because she thought he might absent-mindedly eat along with her. But it was love's labor lost.

While she was shoving her veal goulash around with her fork, a guest at one of the other tables suddenly jumped up. He resoundingly boxed the ears of a newsboy who was going the rounds with the latest evening edition. "What's got into you?" the gentleman yelled. "Put my matchbox back on the table at once!"

"Bravo!" cried someone at the next table. "I should have given him a good slap, too!"

"He tried the same thing on me!" cried a third. "Waiter, bring the manager here immediately. He'll take care of this!"

There was quite an uproar. The newsboy was holding his cheek. The guests were holding the newsboy. The headwaiter brought the manager. The manager signaled to a bellboy. The bellboy brought a policeman from the street corner. The policeman drew his notebook out of his pocket.

"I've no idea what's got into all of you!" the newsboy complained. "We hear all the time on the radio that the public should be on the lookout because the Little Man has been kidnapped! And then when one *is* on the lookout and sets an example by peeping into strangers' matchboxes to see if the Little Man is perhaps hidden inside, one gets one's ears boxed. I don't like that sort of thing, officer!"

No sooner had the guests and the policeman heard this than they were all filled with remorse and contrition. They all apologized to one another. And even the newsboy was no longer angry. In a twinkling he sold all his evening newspapers from the sack hung around his neck, and departed satisfied. The policeman was invited to have a glass of beer on the house.

Everywhere one looked, there was someone studying the evening paper. Although it was the latest edition, there was nothing new in it about Maxie. Nevertheless, a reporter had written a short article about the unsolved crime. All the guests at "The Golden Ham" were reading it, and letting their food grow cold. Rosa Marzipan and Hokus, too, leaning close together, were reading the newspaper. The article was on the top right hand side of the front page:

142

LITTLE MAN MYSTERY

Where is he? Where has he been hidden? On what street? In which house? Which room? An entire city is holding its breath. An entire city is helpless. Detective Inspector Steinbeiss shrugs his shoulders. He and his men are looking haggard. What have they found so far? A waiter's white jacket in a trash can. And the shop where the white jacket was purchased.

What else? Nothing. What did the purchaser look like? Was it "the false waiter?" Or was it an accomplice? Did the criminal who kidnapped our Little Man get into a waiting car? Did he lose himself among the crowds strolling on the pavements?

The criminal police are ceaselessly investigating hundreds of leads that have come in by telephone and by letter from all levels of the population. The work is colossal. The effort is staggering. The result—nothing. Nevertheless we should not relax our vigilance.

Even though a thousand clues lead to nothing, our trouble would be richly rewarded if the thousand and first clue helped to bring back to us, safe and sound, the Little Man, that darling of the public.

Yes, it was bad. Very bad. No one knew the street, the house, and the room where Maxie was being held prisoner. And what a lot of streets, houses, and rooms there are in a city with more than a million inhabitants!

143

Not even Maxie himself knew where he was. He only knew the room in which Bernard and bald, drunken Otto were guarding him. And that was one of those cheaply furnished rooms which resemble one another like ready-made suits. But, even if it had been a room with Venetian mirrors and a self-portrait by Goya on the walls, what use would that have been to the Little Man? That would not have told him the number of the house and the name of the street.

In one respect he knew more than Hokus, Rosa Marzipan, the police, the circus, and the rest of the world: he knew without a doubt that he was still alive and in good health! That was something the rest of the world did not know. And Maxie was very worried lest Hokus should be very worried about him. Yes, it was really bad. Very bad.

When Bernard returned, the two crooks watched him like hawks. Usually the pair of them. They never left him alone for even half a second. At night it was the same thing. One would always be sitting beside his matchbox keeping guard over him. They took turns going out to eat. And, in order not to attract attention, they ate in a different restaurant every day.

Otto fried and boiled Maxie's tiny meals on a propane gas stove. He made a pretty bad job of it, although he tried rather hard. "Now eat it all up," he would always say. "Because if you fall sick or kick the bucket, Lopez'll have our lights and our livers."

"But who *is* this Señor Lopez?" Maxie asked.

"Don't you go sticking your nose into other people's business!" Otto gruffly replied, and blinked at him angrily with his red-rimmed little eyes.

Maxie smiled and was silent. Then he said suddenly, "Please open the window. It's stuffy in here. I need some fresh air."

Groaning, Otto stood up, opened the window, and sat down again.

After a while Maxie pretended to be freezing. "I'm freezing. Please close the window!"

Groaning, Otto stood up again, closed the window, and sat down again.

Five minutes later Maxie asked, "Is there still a bit of the pineapple tart left?"

Groaning, Otto stood up, looked into the cabinet, sat down again, and grunted, "No. You've gobbled it all up."

"Please go to the bakery and bring me another one!"

"No!" bawled Otto, making the walls shake. "No!" he bellowed, "you little varmint!" Then he thought to himself that he was responsible for Maxie's well being, pulled himself together, and declared, as gently as he could, "I'll bring you one when Bernard's come back from lunch."

"Many thanks," said Maxie in a friendly way, and waited tensely for something to happen—for someone to knock on the door or ring the bell or for someone in the house to come angrily inquiring why there was all this frightful row at noon. For this was the only reason he was now provoking bald Otto to become white with rage! Let the fellow bellow! As if he were on a spit, roasting slowly!

"Remarkable," the Little Man thought to himself. "After all, there must be a whole house attached to these two rooms. . . . And, after all, in a house there are people living . . . but no one knocks and no one rings. . . . Where *can* I be?" He did not show what he was feeling. But deep inside he was terribly afraid. Can you understand that? He acted cool as a cucumber. Yet he was shaking like a leaf.

145

He was most afraid of Bernard, because *he* never bellowed. His voice rang as chill as if it had just been brought out of the refrigerator. Whenever he spoke, one froze. And Maxie took care not to provoke him. Fortunately Bernard was frequently away from the house. When he came back, Otto would always ask, "Anything new?" And Bernard mostly answered, "No." Or, "If there's anything new I'll be telling you about it." Or, "Shut your trap!" Or, "Go on! Go and eat! Get out!"

Only once did Otto blow his top with Bernard. He bellowed, "I'm sick and tired of sticking around this dump and playing nurse-maid to a dwarf! When in creation are we going to hit the trail?"

Bernard looked Otto up and down as if he were an old chained watchdog. Then he said, "We are to wait until the cops are not so jumpy. Might be a couple of days more or so."

"What a drag!" Otto complained. "If I had my way, we'd not be sitting here."

Bernard nodded. "That's so! If you had your way, we'd be sitting in the clink."

Otto slurped his glass of brandy empty, stood up groaning, and shoved off grumbling to his lunch. Now Bernard lowered himself into the empty chair and read the newspaper with a bored look.

After a while Maxie asked, putting on a face as innocent as the flowers in May, "Where are we going on our trip?"

"Sometimes I'm a bit hard of hearing," Bernard answered, without lowering the newspaper.

"If that's all," the boy said, "I can speak louder!" And at once he yelled and screamed, "Where are we going on our trip?"

At that, Bernard slowly put down the newspaper. "I've got you now," he said slowly. He was green with fury. "But don't try anything more, you little dwarf. No one can hear you here." He picked his paper up again. "All the same, I advise you to watch your step. Because it's my job to deliver you alive. Alive and as well as possible. I'll get a tidy bit of cash for that. And so it's up to me to see you don't get sick or get stepped on with my heel? You get me?"

"More or less," said Maxie, and endeavored to stop his teeth from chattering.

"At any rate, if you try to pull anything on me, I'll cut my losses. Many a bigger dwarf than you has suddenly died."

Maxie got goose flesh all over.

"So you be a good kid," Bernard went on, "and think about your precious health." Then he opened the newspaper again and began to read the sports news.

Maxie's worries and cares were getting bigger and bigger. The police and Hokus couldn't find him. The higher reward had led to nothing. And he himself no longer knew what to think.

147

At night, while bald Otto lay sleeping on the couch, he had naturally explored the room. He had clambered down the tablecloth and up the curtain to the window. What had he seen? On the other side of the street a row of houses. In the distance a church tower. And the window was bolted.

He had crawled around the floor and had thoroughly examined the walls and above all the door frames. But nowhere was there the slightest chink through which he might have squeezed himself. And what would have happened next, anyhow, if he had found himself standing in the corridor? There would be more doors. The door of the apartment. The door of the house. Those two at least.

But it was pretty useless to think about chinks that did not exist. He was stuck in that confounded room as immovably as a nail in the wall. And time was passing and could not be halted. Soon the two villains, whose Christian names alone he knew, would be sitting in some airplane with an unobtrusive matchbox in Bernard's jacket pocket.

And in the matchbox there would be no matches. Instead it would contain, nicely chloroformed for a few hours, a certain Maxie Pichelsteiner, the celebrated Little Man, who never again would be seen or heard of in the world. The world would never hear of him again and, what was worse, neither would the famous conjurer and circus performer, Professor Hokus von Pokus.

Maxie ground his teeth. "I must get a move on," he thought. "I must get out of this room. As quickly as possible. No ideas? Am I too stupid for that? That *would* be a joke!"

·19·

Detailed report on Señor Lopez · The castle in South America · Pictures by Remembring and Inkasso · Plane tickets for Friday · Stomach-ache, not quite genuine · Bald Otto runs to the drugstore · Maxie sits on a garden gate

Wednesday was an eventful day. By mid-morning Otto was already quite tipsy and started throwing out bits of free information about the mysterious Señor Lopez. Later Bernard came back from town, showed Otto the flight tickets for Friday which he had just bought, but went out again immediately, because he was hungry. "I'll be eating at 'The Loaded Dice,' " he said, "and I'll come and relieve you in an hour."

"All right," said Otto. "If they have pickled pork and sauerkraut, ask them to reserve just *two* portions for me. I'm not hungry today."

When Bernard had gone, Maxie suddenly got a frightful stomach-ache and whimpered and wailed so much that Otto covered his ears. But I think it would be better if first of all I were to tell you in greater detail what bald Otto had related about the mysterious Señor Lopez a few hours earlier.

Well, Otto was already drunk at breakfast. Full right up to the top. Perhaps he had mistaken the brandy bottle for the coffee pot—or had gargled with raspberry liqueur by mistake. At any rate, he began, unasked, "That Lopez, he's a crazy guy. Señor means Mister. A crazy mister, that guy is. Richer than the Bank of England. On every finger two or three rings. Just give me one of them rings and I could buy the whole of Switzerland! But what would *I* do with Switzerland? Ah well, it doesn't matter. The fourth third at least of South America belongs to Lopez! Copper and tin and coffee beans and silver mines and haci . . . haci . . . haciendas with nothing but cattle, from pasture to corned beef, one, two, one, two, into the cans! Has a kind of castle down there. Between Santiago and Valparaiso. With its own airport and a hundred snipers who could shoot a cigar clean out of the hand of a common housefly."

That was too much for Maxie. He tittered.

"That's enough of that!" Otto growled. "That Lopez is nothing to laugh at. It just seems so. Whenever any of these oil paintings worth a million gets swiped, it's hanging next week in his under-ground gallery. Could be a genu-ine Adolf Dürer or a Remembring or one of these modernistic painters such as the celebrated Inkasso. . . ."

"Picasso," Maxie corrected, "and Rembrandt and Albrecht Dürer."

150

"The same difference," Otto said, and stowed the next glass of brandy away behind his belt buckle. "The main thing to remember is, them pictures is hanging in his basement, Lopez' basement. Not a soul knows about them. Not even Interpol. And even if *they* knew about them, they couldn't do nothing. The sharpshooters wouldn't even let them into the castle."

"What *is* Interpol?" Maxie asked.

"It's an abbreviation for . . . for . . . for International Police. They once very nearly got their hands on Bernard and me! When we'd lifted the gypsy fortuneteller and were waiting at Lisbon Airport to fly her across in Lopez' private plane. But it worked out, in the end. She's been two years down there in his castle laying out the cards for him every day. Like whether he should buy stocks on the Stock Exchange just then or not. Or whether one of his race horses will come in first . . . ."

"And what on earth would he want with me?" Maxie asked tensely.

"Why did he want you to steal *me* this time and fly me across to him?"

Otto poured himself another glass. The bottle was almost empty. He knocked the brandy back, coughed, snuffled, and said, "The man's bored, and that's why he's collecting things. People as well as pictures. Like they was stamps. Money's no object. He had a whole ballet troupe abducted. Have to dance something for him every evening. Do you think Lopez'll let them go? No dice. They'd denounce him straight away. Am I right, or am I right? And he's got a famous professor locked up there as well. Because he can tell if an expensive picture's genu-ine or false."

"And what if the professor were to deceive him?"

"He tried it on once." Otto grinned. "It wasn't good for his health, I can tell you. Lopez don't like to be made a fool of."

"But *what* does he want with *me?*" Maxie asked, in a trembling voice.

"Haven't the slightest. He wants you, so he'll get you, and that's that! Maybe because you're a freak. Like a calf with two or three heads."

Maxie stared at Otto's protruberant ears. "A face like a pot with two handles," he thought. And then another thought came uppermost in his mind, "I must get away from here! Time's getting short!"

I've already mentioned that at this point Bernard turned up. "We're flying on Friday," he said, and showed the flight tickets. He didn't stay long because he wanted to lunch at "The Loaded Dice" and relieve Otto within an hour, though the bald one didn't feel really hungry. Two portions of pickled pork with sauerkraut, he had said, would be enough for him.

"Bernard'll be coming back in an hour," thought Maxie. "So it's action stations! He's already got the plane tickets. It's now or never!" And so the Little Man suddenly got an acute stomach-ache and started whimpering and screaming until Otto had to put his hands over his pot handles, I mean his ears.

"Ah-ah-ow-ow!" he groaned. "Oh-oh-oh-oh!" he yowled. "Oo-oo-oo-oo-ooh!" he howled, and writhed like a worm in his matchbox. "Get a doctor!" he shrieked. "At once! Ow-ow-ow-ow! Quickly! Quickly!"

"Where am I going to find a doctor?" Otto asked, worried.

"Get a doctor!" the boy bellowed. "Get one! Now!"

"Are you right off your rocker?" Otto cried. "The whole city's looking for you, and here you are asking me to drag a doctor into the house and have him get us arrested?"

"Ow-ow-ow-ow!" yelled Maxie, throwing himself from side to side. "Help! I'm dying!"

"Don't you dare!" Otto yelled back. "That would be the last straw! There's going to be no dying here. Lopez would wring our necks if we arrived without you!" The bald one was almost in tears. "Where've you *got* this pain?"

Maxie held his stomach. "Here!" he whimpered. "Oh-oh-oh-oh! It's—Ow!—stomach cramp! I often get it. Oo-oo-oo-oooh! Quick, a doctor! Or else—Ee-ee-ee-ee!—get me some medicine—some valerian drops!" He was howling like eight hyenas at night.

"Valerian drops?" Otto groaned, and wiped his handkerchief over his face. "Where the dickens am I going to get valerian drops?"

"Drugstore!" screamed Maxie. "Quick! Quick! Ah-ow-ow-ow!"

"But I can't leave this room just now!" screamed Otto. "Take a glass of brandy! It's medicine too!" He lifted the bottle. It was empty.

"Drugstore!" Maxie moaned. "Otherwise I'll . . ." He sank back groaning, gasping for breath, then lay still as a log.

Otto squinted alarmed at the matchbox. He was at his wits' end. "Have you fainted?"

"Not quite yet," Maxie whispered. He fluttered his eyelids and made his teeth chatter a bit.

"I'll shut the door and run to a drugstore and come back in a jiffy!"

"Yes, hurry!"

Otto jammed on his hat, ran out of the room, gave the key a double turn in the lock, put the key in his trouser pocket, stumbled along the corridor, flung open the door of the apartment, slammed it behind him, locked it, put this second key also in his trouser pocket, and staggered downstairs.

Out of the house, through the front garden, and through the iron garden gate. He was looking for a drugstore, or at least for some shop selling aspirins, and so on.

"Valerian drops for the dwarf," he was groaning. "And a bottle of brandy for poor old Otto."

The room was locked. Until Otto returned, no one could enter and
no one could get out. Not even Maxie could get out. But that was
no longer necessary.

Eh? *Why* was that no longer necessary? Don't you know why?
Surely you must have guessed already. No? Well, then, listen! It
was no longer necessary, quite simply because Maxie was no longer

in the room. He had left it at the same time as Otto! But how? On Otto's back, of course! That was the plan which he had thought out for himself!

The Little Man had never believed that Otto would bring a doctor. Not for one second. But this was part of his plan. The bald one would much rather run to a drugstore, Maxie had reasoned. And that was exactly what had happened.

When Otto had taken his hat from the peg, he had turned his back on the matchbox—and, at once, Maxie, making a soundless leap, had landed on Otto's jacket and climbed up. For a famous artiste this was child's play.

And while Otto had been locking the room door and going down the stairs and out of the house and locking the house door and running through the front garden, Maxie had all the time been clinging to Otto's shoulder.

On reaching the garden gate, Maxie had jumped across to one of the iron bars. Not a hitch. Training tells. His forehead hurt a little. Cast iron is not rubber. Probably he would have a bruise or a bump or even both. No matter!

Maxie was now sitting on one of the two high stone posts on either side of the garden gate, each one of which was topped by a stone ball. He sat up there and took a deep breath. The air smelled of jasmine. And it smelled of freedom, too!

Maxie was in raptures. But this was not the right time for jasmine and raptures. He must get away from here. He must push on. Otto would not be away for long! In less than an hour Bernard would come back from "The Loaded Dice!" Every minute was as precious as a whole year in more peaceful times.

The street was empty, as if there were no more people left on earth. The houses on the other side stood silent.

Maxie turned around and looked up at the door of the house through which, shortly before, Otto had stumbled out bearing him on his shoulder. Next to the door hung a blue plate with a white number on it. And under the number stood, in small white letters, the name of the street.

"Kickelhahnstrasse 12," Maxie murmured. "12 Kickelhahn Street." Just as he was saying it to himself for the third time, a window opened on the first floor of a house opposite. Then a boy leaned out over the window sill, took a brown paper bag of cherries out of his pocket, and started putting one cherry after another in his mouth and spitting the stones out into the street. He was aiming at a small green child's ball lying there, and wasn't doing at all badly.

The cherry-stone spitter gets angry · His name is Jacob · Maxie makes a telephone call and waits for whatever the future may bring · Cars 1, 2, and 3 · Bald Otto rides in a car · Maxie rides in a car · Jacob rides in a car · The quiet street is quiet again

"Hello, there!" Maxie called.

But the boy at the window took no notice and went on practicing his shots. It was not all that easy to hit the green ball with a cherry stone. Sailors maybe could have done it. (As every child knows, those fellows must be champion spitters. When they become helmsmen and captains that skill decreases somewhat. Probably it's a question of age.)

"Hello, there!" Maxie called even louder.

The boy glanced across the street, but as he could see no one he went on carefully spitting out stones.

Maxie was getting uneasy. Time was passing. What could he do? How could he make the boy get a move on? Fortunately he got an idea which promised to be very successful. "I'll call him names," he thought, "until he really begins to see red."

So again he shouted, "Helloooo!" and then, as the boy did not react, but simply stuck another cherry in his mouth, he cried, "Are you deaf, you old blockhead?"

The boy started, accidentally swallowing a cherry stone, and stared grimly in Maxie's direction. Where was the pest with that fresh voice?

"Don't be such a sissy!" Maxie bellowed. "Or your parents'll take you back to be changed at the next sale!"

At that, the boy swung his legs over the window sill. "That's going a bit too far!" he blurted out. "A joke's a joke!" He hopped down to the pavement, came tearing across the street, stopped in front of the garden gate, doubled his fists aggressively, and couldn't see a soul anywhere. "Come out, you coward!" he yelled, angrily. "Come out of the bushes, you pest! I'll squash you between the palms of my hands!"

Maxie had to laugh at that.

The boy raised his head, discovered Maxie leaning against the stone ball on the top of the pillar, and gaped, flabbergasted, at him. He was going to say something but he couldn't utter a sound.

"Do you know who I am?" Maxie asked.

The boy nodded eagerly.

"Will you help me?"

The boy nodded even more eagerly. His eyes were sparkling.

"I *had* to annoy you like that," Maxie explained, "otherwise you would never have come down. Sorry."

The boy nodded again. Or rather, he was just about to nod but he finally managed to say something, "Don't mention it, Little Man," he said. "Let's forget it. My name is Jacob."

"I'm called Maxie. Have you a telephone?"

Jacob nodded.

"Hold your hand up!" Maxie commanded. "But mind you, don't squash me between the palms of your hands!"

Jacob blushed deep red but held his hand as high as he could. Maxie jumped down from the pillar. Right into the middle of the open hand.

Jacob dashed across the street, sat the Little Man on the window sill, climbed the wall, and swung himself into the room. Then he took hold of Maxie again and ran to a desk. A telephone was standing on it.

"Whom do you want to call?" Jacob asked.

"The Criminal Investigation Bureau," said Maxie. "Because if I call Hokus at the hotel—but you don't know Hokus."

"Excuse me!" replied Jacob. "Of course I know Professor Hokus von Pokus! I know both of you from the circus and TV and newspapers and everything!"

"Because if I call Hokus he'll come at once and wring bald Otto's neck. And then Bernard's. That would only complicate matters."

"I've got you," Jacob said. "Otto and Bernard are the kidnappers." He looked at a newspaper cutting sticking in the blotter. "Here is the police message. With their telephome number and all."

"Very good, Jacob," said Maxie, and rubbed his hands with glee. "As soon as you've got someone on the line, lay the receiver on the desk, will you? Then I can talk to them myself."

Jacob dialed the telephone number and said after a while, "Please connect me with Detective Inspector Steinbeiss! He's busy? That's a pity. Well, give him the Little Man's very best wishes!" Jacob grinned at Maxie and murmured, "That shook him! The policeman nearly had a stroke!"

Three seconds later a voice boomed out of the telephone; it sounded as if the detective were standing right in the middle of the room. "Steinbeiss here! What *is* it?"

Maxie knelt in front of the mouthpiece and shouted, "This is the Little Man speaking! Maxie Pichelsteiner! I've escaped! From house number 12, Kickelhahn Street! Otto will be back soon! Now I'm in the house opposite . . ."

"Number 17," Jacob hurriedly whispered. "Name Hurtig. First floor left."

"House number 17, name Hurtig, first floor left! Do you understand? Just a minute, I must run to the earpiece."

Maxie ran to the earpiece.

"We'll be with you right away," the detective inspector called. "Meanwhile, be careful! Anything else?"

Maxie leaped back to the mouthpiece and, in his excitement, almost stuck his head into it, "Please don't use your sirens and warning lights. Otto is still at the drugstore and would be warned away! And the most important important thing, Defective Injector, I mean Dejected Infector, I mean . . . Oh, I'm all mixed-up! *Don't* say anything to Hokus! Not yet, not yet! Please, please, and please once again! He gets worked-up so easily! Is he all right? And Rosa Marzipan, too? And . . ."

Jacob held the receiver to his ear and signaled to Maxie that they had been cut off. "All quiet on the western front. Probably the valiant officers of the law have just jumped from the third floor straight into their patrol cars. With twenty pistols in their holsters."

"More haste, less speed," Maxie said. "Please carry me to the window!"

Jacob laid the telephone receiver back on the rest. "It will be a great honor for me, Herr von Pichelsteiner."

They sat at the open window and waited impatiently for whatever the future would bring. Who would be the first to reach the house? Detective Inspector Steinbeiss and his men? Or bald Otto with the valerian drops?

Jacob again was spitting cherry stones at the green ball and still had not quite got his range. "Spitting at a target is difficult," he stated. "Almost as difficult as life itself."

"And why is life more difficult?" Maxie asked.

162

"My dear sir," the other boy sighed. "It's a sad story—father away, mother away, son feeding himself on fruit. What could be worse?"

"When did they abandon you?" Maxie asked, deeply shocked.

"Early this morning."

"For good?"

"Not altogether. They'll be back tomorrow evening."

They both burst out laughing.

"Aunt Anna," Jacob informed Maxie, "has had a baby and I couldn't talk my parents out of going to see her."

"And they left only a bag of cherries here for you?"

"Heaven forbid!" Jacob said in insulted tones. "I had enough cash to fill three wallets. I was to have eaten at restaurants. This noon and this evening and tomorrow noon. But . . ."

"But what?"

"As I was going into school, I saw Fritz Griebitz standing outside crying. He was carrying his little dachshund in his arms. His dog always ran with him to the school gates and then back home. Puffi had been run over by a car."

"Oh," Maxie murmured.

"So we collected some money. For the funeral and for Puffi number two. And when we came into the classroom, the teacher looked at the clock. Boy, did he give us a sour look! And now I only have a few cents left until tomorrow evening. . . . And nothing but cherries. . . . Now, is life difficult, or isn't it?"

Maxie nodded understandingly. He was nibbling and gnawing at a cherry which he was holding in both hands. It looked as if he were trying to lift a giant pumpkin that had won the Gold Medal at the

World's Fair. And he said, "Hold on a little longer, Jacob, and we'll both be eating pineapple tarts."

"Fruit again!" said Jacob despondently.

Detective Inspector Steinbeiss and Inspector Muller came walking rapidly along Kickelhahn Street. Three cars with the rest of the men were waiting, just around the corner in Three Stars Lane.

"That's number 12 over there," the inspector murmured. "That's where he was held prisoner."

"Very quiet street," the detective inspector said. Then he grabbed his cheek. "Who's that shooting cherry stones?"

"Excuse me, sir!" a boy shouted. "I was trying to hit that green ball."

"Since when do I look like a green ball?" the detective inspector grumbled.

"Number 17, first floor left," Inspector Muller whispered. "This is it."

The detective inspector went to the open window. "Are you called Hurtig by any chance?"

"Hurtig, that's right," Jacob replied. "But certainly not 'by any chance.'"

Inspector Muller grinned.

"Criminal Investigation Bureau!" Detective Inspector Steinbeiss grunted. "We've come to get the Little Man."

Jacob said, "A lot of people would like to do that. May I see your identification card?"

At first Herr Steinbeiss' fingers twitched convulsively. But then he pulled out his identification card and showed it to the fresh little monkey.

Jacob studied the card thoroughly. "These are the right ones, Maxie," he said.

Only then did Maxie raise his head above the window sill. "Greetings, gentlemen! How is he?"

"Who?"

"Hokus, of course!"

"He's well on the way to being a professional starving man," the detective said drily.

Maxie's face darkened. But only for a second. Then he was radiant again and rubbed his hands. "This evening he's going to eat at least four veal cutlets! I'm looking forward to seeing that already!"

Suddenly they heard hurried, unsteady footsteps!

Maxie climbed on the window sill. "That's bald Otto," he whispered.

Otto was coming along on the other side with rather uncertain, drunken steps, holding a big fat bottle clasped to his breast.

"Is that full of valerian drops?" Jacob asked in astonishment.

Maxie giggled. "That's brandy! His bottle was empty. That's why he ran so fast to the drugstore."

"Well now, let's get moving," Herr Steinbeiss said to Herr Muller.

"One moment!" Maxie whispered. Then he jumped on the detective inspector's sleeve and in a trice had climbed into his breast pocket.

Otto was just going to turn into the garden gate of Number 12 when they barred his way. "What's up?" he asked furiously, and gave the two men a nasty look.

"Criminal Investigation Bureau," the detective inspector said. "You are under arrest."

"Oh-ho! You don't say so!" Otto mocked, and turned to run away.

But Herr Muller was too fast for him. He tackled Otto firmly. "Ow!" yelled Otto, and let his big bottle fall. It smashed. Herr Steinbeiss blew on his policeman's whistle. Three cars came out of Three Stars Lane and stopped. Six plain-clothes officers jumped out on the pavement.

"Patrol car No. 1 will take the arrested man at once to the police station," the detective inspector ordered. "The inspector will take the men from patrol car No. 2 and search the house and the apartment."

"Second floor on the left," said Maxie. "Otto has the keys in his right-hand trouser pocket." And at once an officer was fishing out the keys.

Bald Otto blinked, as if struck by lightning, at the detective inspector's breast pocket. Then he bellowed, "You little good-for-nothing! How did you get out . . ." But before he could bawl out the end of his sentence, he was sitting, under strong guard, in patrol car No. 1, which immediately drove away!

An officer from car No. 2 announced, "Detective Inspector Steinbeiss, sir! The police radio informed us two minutes ago that house number 12 on Kickelhahn Street belongs to a South American trading company."

"I'm not at all surprised," Maxie remarked. "It all adds up, Señor Lopez and everything."

Inspector Muller asked in amazement, "What do *you* know about Lopez?"

"Not much," replied the Little Man. "But too much to tell you now."

Herr Steinbeiss nodded brusquely. "He's right. We're in a hurry. Car No. 2 take over the house. Car No. 3 will take me and Maxie to the Professor at his hotel."

"No," said Maxie. "We must first go to 'The Loaded Dice' and arrest Bernard while he's having lunch. He's ten times worse than bald Otto. It was he who was the false waiter in the white jacket!"

The detective inspector couldn't help laughing. "Maxie's in charge! Maxie knows everything! Let's get going, car No. 3, to 'The Loaded Dice!' " He shoved himself into the seat next to the driver and felt for his revolver.

"One moment!" Maxie suddenly cried, and leaned right out of the breast pocket. "Car No. 2 must please bring my matchbox with them! Otherwise I'll have to sleep in my awful 'heavenly bed' to-night."

"That would be really dreadful," said Inspector Muller, as he left to storm into the house with his men.

"What are we waiting for?" the detective inspector asked the driver of car No. 3. "Let's get going!"

"I can't get going!" the driver informed him. "There's a boy standing on the running board!"

Jacob was looking through the car window. "Am I invited to have some pineapple tart or not?"

Maxie heaved a sigh, as if it were his very last, or at least the one before the very last. "I should be heartily ashamed of myself," he stammered. "I've barely got myself out of this mess, and already I'm forgetting my best friends!"

Jacob Hurtig quickly got into the car. "Don't give it a thought!"

Patrol car No. 1 was on its way to the police station with bald Otto. Patrol car No. 3 was now racing towards "The Loaded Dice." Patrol car No. 2 was standing in front of 12 Kickelhahn Street and the green ball was again lying as quietly as it was half an hour before.

On the pavement there glittered the fragments of a brandy bottle. Otherwise, it seemed, nothing had changed.

·21·

Uproar in "The Loaded Dice" · Jacob would rather have gone to a "knuckle of veal" hotel · Tears and training · Marzipan with goose flesh · Strong mustard · Who gets the reward? · Maxie mimics bald Otto · What's the smallest five-figure figure?

"The Loaded Dice" was not much of a place, but the food was good. I've nothing against that. If the soup is real meat broth, the plate doesn't have to be of genuine porcelain. Usually it's the other way around.

The customers sat and ate at well-scrubbed tables, and they enjoyed their food. Only Bernard pulled a face, as always. The strapping proprietress, bringing him his dessert, wasn't very surprised. "So it don't taste good again?" she asked grimly.

169

"High time I get to countries where people know how to cook," he retorted.

"High time you don't come back to my place," she snapped, and snatched the dessert away from under his nose. (By the way, it was caramel pudding with raspberry sauce.)

"Bring back that daft, shivery-shaky stuff at once!" he ordered icily. You know what his refrigerator voice was like!

"Take yourself out of here at once!" she calmly replied. "The two portions of pickled pork are being kept for your bald mate. That's the lot. As for *you*—get out! I don't want any money! Kindly consider yourself my guest and leave! Go on, beat it, you horrible vulture you!"

Bernard grabbed the plate in his rage. But the proprietress stepped back and threw it right in his face. Whether one likes caramel pudding with raspberry sauce is a matter of personal taste. I, for one, don't like it. But—plonk—right in your face? Nobody likes it served *that* way. Nevertheless Bernard stuck out his tongue and eagerly lapped up the raspberry sauce trickling down his face. He was afraid it would stain his white shirt and light-gray suit and smart necktie.

The actual pudding—a really excellent pudding—stuck in his hair and gummed up his ice-blue eyes. He groped with all ten fingers in the air and over his face, felt for the napkin, tried to find his handkerchief in his trouser pocket—and all this naturally didn't make things any better.

The customers were laughing. The proprietress was laughing. And when a little girl at the next table cried, "Mommy, the man looks like a pig!" the general merriment knew no bounds.

Yet all of a sudden they were all as still as mice. What had happened?

Bernard squinted through the clammy caramel pudding and gave a start—he had every reason to. For three men were standing around him and seemed to be finding him not funny at all.

The worst thing was that out of one of the men's breast pocket leaned a familiar little figure which pointed to Bernard and stated, loud and clear, "Detective Inspector, that is he!"

After they delivered Bernard, still all gummed-up, to the police station, Maxie was to be driven back to his hotel. Jacob Hurtig remained standing outside the car and declared, "I don't want to disturb you any longer."

"You're coming with me!" said Maxie. "For the pineapple tart and everything."

"Of course you're coming with us!" the detective inspector said. "After all, I have to write down your personal details and everything."

"That's O.K. by me," Jacob replied. "After all, my parents are at Aunt Anna's seeing to the stork and everything!"

The three of them laughed, and were driven speedily back to the hotel.

Inspector Muller had telephoned beforehand. And so the entire staff was there, from the manager to the bellboys and elevator operators all waiting in the lobby to shout, "Long shall he live! Long shall he live! Three cheers!" The telephone operators were waving huge sheaves of flowers in the air. And the pastry chef presented Maxie with a pineapple tart. It was as big as the spare tire of a long-distance truck.

"There now, what did I tell you?" The Little Man said to Jacob. "Pineapple tart!"

Jacob pulled a face. "Don't they have anything else here? Is this a pineapple-tart hotel? I would definitely prefer a knuckle-of-veal hotel."

Maxie beckoned to the manager. "Have you any knuckles of veal today?"

"At least three dozen," the manager said. "Tender as butter."

"How many do you want?" Maxie asked.

"One will do," said Jacob. "If possible, with potato salad."

"Very well. One knuckle of veal with potato salad for the young gentleman," the manager repeated the order.

"No, no!" said Jacob. "For *me!*"

Rosa Marzipan went up in the elevator with Maxie. She held the Little Man firmly in both hands and pressed his face gently against her marzipan cheek.

"Does he know?" Maxie asked.

She nodded and said, "Five minutes ago. But he didn't want to come down into the lobby."

The elevator stopped. Rosa went along the corridor, knocked, and cried gaily, "Here we are!"

The door opened. The Professor spread wide both his arms and cried, "Come in, both of you!" He sounded as if he had a cold in the nose.

Rosa smiled and shook her head. "I don't like to see men weeping.

I'll come back for you in one hour." Then she carefully placed the Little Man in Hokus' hand, dropped a deep curtsey, and ran back to the elevator. She was gone.

When she put her ear to the door one hour later, that ear received no small surprise. There was no longer any trace of weeping to be heard. Instead, Rosa heard cries of command. And as she cautiously opened the door she saw Maxie scrambling about on Winsome Waldemar. He was in training again!

"Faster, my boy!" Hokus ordered him. "More smoothly! Oh, you've gotten fat! You must get rid of that potbelly! What must you get rid of?"

"My potbelly!"

"What must you get rid of?"

"My potbelly!" Maxie said, chortled, and disappeared inside Waldemar's necktie. Soon he had loosed the knot and Maxie, guided unfailingly by Hokus' hand, slithered with the tie down into the latter's left pocket.

Winsome Waldemar went on staring steadily ahead and not noticing anything. Rosa peeped through the open door. "Hooray, the artistes!" she cried, and clapped her hands. Emma and Minna, the two doves, were hopping backwards and forwards along the top of the wardrobe, fluttering their wings with excitement.

"Two more training sessions, and he'll be fit," Hokus said in a satisfied voice. "We can perform again on Friday."

Maxie popped his head out of the Professor's pocket, like a jack-in-the-box. "That's impossible, Your Honor! On Friday I'm flying to join Señor Lopez in South America with bald Otto and pudding-face Bernard!"

"What desperate sounding names!" cried Rosa. "They give me goose flesh all over."

Maxie rubbed his hands. "Show me! Marzipan with goose flesh all over is something I'd very much like to see, just once!"

Rosa winked at Hokus. "Life in the criminal fraternity unfortunately seems to have rubbed off on Herr Pichelsteiner somewhat. He has become frivolous."

Hokus fished Maxie out of his pocket. "I'll put him in King Bileam's bath. Cleanliness is next to godliness."

175

They had dinner in the Blue Salon and it was to everyone's satisfaction, even Jacob's, though tears came to his eyes when he got to the veal knuckles. But this was caused only by the strong English mustard which he was tasting for the first time. "We live and learn," he said, wafting cool air with his napkin into his open mouth.

Hokus did not eat four veal cutlets, only two. And even that took time. For there were so many things to talk about. For example, they talked with Herr Brausewetter about the circus performance on Friday. At intervals they talked with the reporters outside the dining room and on the telephone. And not least they talked with Detective Inspector Steinbeiss, who, late though it was, came over from the police station.

The others were already eating their dessert. "Oh, pineapple tarts!" Detective Inspector Steinbeiss said enthusiastically. "My favorite dish!" And then he polished off three immensely big portions.

At first Maxie and Jacob thought that this was very comical, the detective inspector liking pineapple tarts. But they soon became serious again. For Hokus asked the detective inspector during his second piece of pineapple tart, "Now who is actually the person to receive the reward I offered?"

"Jacob!" Maxie cried. "It's as clear as day!"

"Me? Why me?" Jacob spoke up. "Certainly not! If Maxie had not teased me in so beastly a way, I should still be sitting at the window, same as before, unaware of anything. You might just as well give your money to bald Otto in jail. For after all, it was *he* who freed Maxie!"

"Yes, but without knowing he was doing so," Herr Brausewetter stated. "He intended to buy valerian drops, that was all."

"And what did I intend to do?" Jacob Hurtig asked. "I only intended to punch some bigmouth on the nose."

"And squash him between the palms of your hands!" Maxie cried, laughing. He was sitting on the table and allowing Rosa to feed him with bits of pineapple tart.

"Another little morsel?" she asked.

But the detective inspector was already shoving back his plate and saying briskly, "It was thanks to the Little Man himself that he was not abducted abroad. He was at one and the same time the missing person and the finder. If anyone can prove the contrary to me, then I'm a street cleaner."

Well, the others did not want to have any part in bringing about such a drastic change of occupation. And therefore nobody spoke, and the party went on as merrily as ever. Maxie stole the show. He mimicked bald Otto. He staggered about the table between plates and cups and all the time related the major part of what that drunken old rascal Otto had told him about Señor Lopez. He told all about the castle in South America, the underground art gallery, the gypsy fortuneteller, the bodyguard of snipers, and the poor ballet dancers.

The only person who did not laugh outright at Maxie's masterly performance, but only occasionally grinned, was Detective Inspector Steinbeiss. He took down in shorthand everything the Little Man uttered. Then he slammed his notebook shut and hurriedly departed. "I must spend a few more hours questioning the two villains," he said.

"Even Interpol is helpless where Lopez is concerned!" Maxie shouted after him. "The fellow's much too rich!"

The detective inspector, who had already reached the door, started and turned around. "He's little, but oh-ho . . . !" he said appreciatively. "What about it? Would you like to be my assistant?"

Maxie gave him a gracious bow. "No, thank you, Detective Inspector. I am, and shall always remain, an artiste."

When Jacob Hurtig was hurtling into bed that night, he tossed his jacket over the chair and heard a sound of paper rustling in the inside pocket. There he discovered a certified check made out in his name, read the amount, whispered, "good grief!" and sat down on the edge of the bed.

There was also a note. It read:

Dear Jacob,
Heartiest thanks for your help.
Your new friends, Maxie and Hokus.

It was a five-figure amount. And although it was only the smallest five-figure sum, it was still a large sum of money for a boy whose father was district representative for a sectional furniture company.

(Incidentally—what *is* the smallest possible five-figure sum?)

When Hokus came back with Maxie into their hotel room, the good old matchbox was lying there on the bedside table. And under the cover lay a note. It read:

Dear Little Man,
Herewith, as per orders, your own bed from Kickelhahn Street.
Muller, Police Inspector.

Maxie rubbed his hands and said, "Now I have all I want."

·22·

Why the Gala Performance lasted twenty-seven minutes longer · Herr Brausewetter reads out three telegrams · Jacob temporarily loses his temper · The police take a bow · Entry of the chief characters · Rejoicing without end ·
END

On Friday, of course, Ringmaster Brausewetter was really in his element. Once more an evening after his own heart! He would have liked to pull on three snow-white pairs of kid gloves one over the other, and to wear two top hats! It was, in any case, a Gala Performance that would be well worth seeing. He understood that kind of thing, did our Ringmaster Brausewetter, Donnerbrausewetter rather! (Or do you like "Brausedonnerwetter" better?)

The program lasted twenty-seven minutes longer than usual, but this was not the fault of the lions or the elephants or the artistes. They all performed with their usual precision. There were two other reasons.

First, Ringmaster Brausewetter read out a few of the most important telegrams of congratulation that Maxie had received. I can still remember three of them very well. The Gymnastic Association in Pichelstein had wired:

```
TELEGRAM
   MAXIE PICHELSTEINER
   STILKE'S CIRCUS
   132 PICHELSTEIN T 13     BERLIN  =
GREETINGS AND BLESSINGS  STOP  WE WERE
STANDING VIGILANTLY IN STANDING-IN POSITION
AS FOR A GRAND CIRCLE WITH SPLITS FINISH
STOP  BRAVO  STOP  ARE PROUD OF YOU  STOP

   ALL PICHELSTEINERS IN PICHELSTEIN
3    COL 13 15 +      7773AC PICH T
```

The second telegram had come from the Kingdom of Breganzona. It made a deep impression on the audience. Because there are not many kings left nowadays. So one must make the most of them and be thankful for any sign of life. The telegram read:

```
TELEGRAM
   FROM 111 BREGANZONA K 1435
   MAXIE PICHELSTEINER
   STILKE'S CIRCUS        BERLIN =
WERE FRIGHTFULLY WORKED UP  STOP  FIRST
WITH WORRY NOW WITH JOY  STOP  SAFETY CHAIN
FOR HOTEL ROOM DOOR FOLLOWS EXPRESS AIRMAIL
STOP  COME AND VISIT US IN BREGANZONA   STOP
NICE CASTLE NICE PEOPLE  STOP  OUR GREETINGS
ALSO TO PROFESSOR HOKUS STOP  =

   YOUR KING BILEAM AND ALL HIS FAMILY
   AND PEOPLE +
BREGONZ L ------------      COL 13 15 +
```

The third cable I remember came from Hollywood. The film company which I have already mentioned cabled this:

```
TELEGRAM
          FROM 1495 HOLLYWOOD F 34 / 36 87 =
     LITTLE MAN
     STILKE'S CIRCUS     BERLIN
     44432 HOLLY F
CONGRATULATIONS ON KIDNAPPING AND SELF
RESCUE   STOP   BRILLIANTLY SUITED TO MOVIE
STOP   DRAFT CONTRACT ON THE WAY   STOP
EUROPEAN REPRESENTATIVE WITH CARTE BLANCHE
ARRIVING MONDAY = +
COL 19 23 = +                        3
```

Second, before the entrance of Maxie and Hokus, Ringmaster Brausewetter introduced the evening's guests of honor who were sitting in three special boxes illuminated by spotlights.

First of all the schoolboy, Jacob Hurtig. He responded to the applause by shaking his clasped hands above his head and bowing in all directions from the waist like a champion boxer who has just knocked out the fearful lumberjack, Paul Bunyan from Minnesota.

Then Jacob again proudly sat down between his parents. "Sit up straight!" his mother hissed at him, and gave him a smack between the shoulder blades. (You know the sort of thing!)

Jacob's face darkened. He jerked away from her and whispered to his father, "Your spouse is unfortunately poisoning the one day of glory of your son who has recently come into a lot of money. Do you consider this proper or improper?"

The elder Hurtig bit his lips. He much admired Jacob's ornate

182

style. And he really couldn't think of an answer. For there was already another burst of applause, because Ringmaster Brausewetter was introducing the crews of the three patrol cars, then Inspector Muller, and finally Detective Inspector Steinbeiss in person.

Scarcely had the applause died away than a group of young people started bellowing for all they were worth, "We want bald Otto! We want pudding-face Bernard! We want the dirty dogs!" And because all the spectators had read the newspapers and listened to the radio, the whole big top shuddered with gales of laughter. It was great fun. Because everybody well knew that Otto and Bernard could not be presented in the circus ring because they were behind bars!

Suddenly Ringmaster Brausewetter made a compelling gesture. And there was sudden stillness, as in the eye of a typhoon. Everyone knew what would be coming next and who would be coming next. You might have heard a pin drop, if a pin had dropped. But no pin dropped.

"And now, ladies and gentlemen!" called Ringmaster Brausewetter, "now at last you are about to see once more, to welcome back and to gaze in wonder at, your and our and everybody's darling, he who is the littlest biggest hero in criminal history, he who is the biggest littlest artiste in the circus world, he and his paternal mentor, Hokus von Pokus, the Professor and Past Master of Applied Magic! Your applause, I already know, will be unprecedented. I ask you not to worry! Anyone who breaks his hands may apply to the box office at the end of the performance for a new pair!"

Brausewetter shot his right arm vertically into the air, like a cavalry general giving the signal for a cavalry charge. Then he galloped, though not on a horse, out of the circus ring.

The orchestra played a deafening fanfare, using all its drums and brass!

And in the entrance to the ring there appeared, immaculate and elegant as ever, Professor Hokus von Pokus. On his outstretched hand stood Maxie, waving and smiling in every direction. What more is there for me to say? Unlike this book, the rejoicing went on without

END